THE LEGEND OF TORNADO TESS

Author Amy Cole wants more than to write a story — she wants to live one. Her chance comes when she's asked to help to clear a doctor of murder. Amy's investigation takes her to Little Babylon, a bandit stronghold in the wasteland of New Mexico. Meanwhile, Whitney Scott trails a band of killers to Little Babylon and meets Amy. However, working together, Whitney faces an unknown assassin — and Amy's priority, over solving the murder, is to stay alive!

Books by Terrell L. Bowers
in the Linford Western Library:

TERRELL L. BOWERS

THE LEGEND OF TORNADO TESS

Complete and Unabridged

LINFORD
Leicester

First published in Great Britain in 2010 by
Robert Hale Limited
London

First Linford Edition
published 2011
by arrangement with
Robert Hale Limited
London

British Library CIP Data

Bowers, Terrell L.
   The legend of Tornado Tess. - -
(Linford western library)
1. Western stories.
2. Large type books.
I. Title II. Series
813.5′4–dc22

ISBN 978–1–44480–549–9

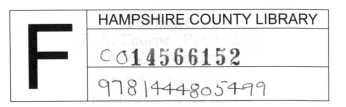

This book is printed on acid-free paper

1

Whitney was returning home from a three-day horse show in Colorado Springs when he saw smoke off in the distance. He first thought it was the cook — an elderly widow, who worked on the Scott ranch — preparing a meal. But the cloud blossomed thick and grayish-black, scorched against the sky like a deadly winter storm. It was far too much smoke to come from a chimney. Something was terribly wrong!

Whitney dug his heels into his horse's flanks. The gelding jumped in surprise, but sprang forward at once into a run, opening up at a gallop, covering the ground with long strides. Although weary from two days of travel, the steed displayed his strength and durability. He kept up the torrid pace a full mile, then a second . . . finally beginning to falter as they topped the last hill before the ranch.

The scene before him instilled a knot of terror in Whitney's chest. Fire raged wild and leapt skyward, ravenously consuming both the house and barn. At least two bodies were sprawled in the yard. Panic-stricken, he couldn't let his horse rest. He had to get down there.

The gelding responded gallantly, though his speed had waned and he was heaving with every bound. When Whitney finally reached the yard, he yanked back on the reins and hit the ground running.

He spied the twisted bodies — two of their three hired hands — lying on the ground near the corral. Of the horses in the pen, one was saddled and another two wore bridles — Greg and Saul had been readying the horses for the day's work. It took only a glance to see they were both dead. He hadn't time to wonder about the fate of their third hired hand, hurrying toward the house. He saw his brother and the elderly cook crumpled on the porch. It appeared Wally had been trying to drag the woman's body out of the house when he collapsed.

The fire blazed and the intense heat drove him back, but he covered his face with his hat and waded in against the heat and smoke. He grabbed Wally by the shirt collar and pulled him away from the burning structure. As he started back for the cook the front wall came crashing down. He had seen blood on the front of her apron and she hadn't moved or made a sound. Instantly buried beneath the fiery timbers, he was reasonably certain — and desperately hoped — she had already been dead.

Wally's exposed skin was blackened and charred from the heat and a hole was in his shirt from where a bullet had hit him in the chest. Whitney carried him to a watering trough and used his bandanna to wet down his younger brother's face. At first, he feared it was too late, that Wally was dead too. But the boy's eyes came open to tiny slits and he recognized Whitney.

'F-four men,' Wally whispered hoarsely. 'Heard . . . ' he swallowed against a spasm of pain and a grimace twisted his face.

'Easy, little brother,' Whitney spoke softly, trying to hold back a sob of grief. 'You'll be all right.' He wet the bandanna again and squeezed a few drops of water into Wally's mouth.

'Overheard a coupla names,' Wally rasped, trying to get the story out. 'Tom and Jack . . . Polson brothers . . . Couldn't . . . '

'We've heard about the three Polson boys before,' Whitney said, assuring him he knew who had attacked the ranch. 'They've been rustling horses and cattle for the last two or three years.'

'G-gave us no chance,' Wally managed the words with difficulty. 'I — ' He coughed up a mouthful of blood, but continued his life's battle. 'I heard shots out in the yard . . . went to see what . . . ' he couldn't continue, his body raked by the pain and torture of impending death.

'I should have been here,' Whitney

4

said. 'I'm sorry.'

His brother's hand squeezed his arm. The last words he managed were, 'G-going to . . . to miss you, big . . . '

As Whitney's eyes filled with tears, his younger brother's face went slack. The light of life vanished from his eyes and a final breath exhaled from his lungs. Surrounded by an inferno of fire, blinding smoke and lingering death, Whitney's tranquil world had been erased from the face of the earth.

* * *

Amanda Cole waved her hand in front of her face, doing little to disturb the endless billowing dust which seeped through the cracks around the windows and pervaded the interior of the cab. Hour upon hour, endless grit boiled up from the hoofs of the team of horses and churning wheels of the stagecoach. The infernal contraption bounced about like a marble rolling over a scrubbing board, flinging Amanda against the side and back of the coach walls from each rut or bump. Worse yet, the silent, foul-smelling drunk — ousted from the last town at gunpoint — kept leaning against her in his besotted stupor. When his body touched hers for about the tenth time, she uttered a cry of frustration and shoved him hard toward the opposite door. He fell over, but his lower body still pressed against her hips and legs. He snorted like the grunt of a pig, tucking his hands under his head and did not even come awake.

Amy, what on earth were you thinking? she wondered. But quickly brushing aside the discomfort and uncertainty, she firmed her resolve.

Tornado Tess could handle any given situation, she reasoned. She is as smart as a fox, brave as a lion, with the cunning of a wolf. Contemplating metaphors of different creatures caused her to smile.

'Tess,' she spoke aloud, 'you sound like a caged animal from a traveling carnival.'

The comfort and security of Saint Louis seemed a lifetime ago, though it was closer to three weeks. Her desire to be involved in realism, actually to live an adventure, had taken her through dozens of cities, ghost towns, mining settlements and farming communities. She had been housed in drafty old shanties, noisy boarding houses and often went several days or more between baths. She had observed men working in every conceivable field, along with wandering bums, shiftless drifters and crooked gamblers. The women she encountered were most often a mixture of angels and soiled doves — either married, with children at their feet, or catering to men, working out of tents or saloons to eke out a dour existence. For all of the excitement she had envisioned in the West, she had yet to meet a single character to instigate a new story.

She questioned her sanity for the journey again, as she had several times each day since leaving the comfortable surroundings of her home and family. There were no policemen at every corner out in this wilderness, no guardian parents at night when she went to bed. The food was foul, the water tepid or alkali and her body felt bruised and it ached from her toenails to the longest strand of hair on her head. This trip was a fool's errand, the silly daydream of a girl with too much imagination.

What am I going to do when I get there? she wondered. *Tess is the intrepid adventuress, the crafty sleuth — not me!*

Amy angrily shook away the doubts. This was a chance to do something real, to make a difference. She had been living through Tess for too long. It was time she —

Her reverie was interrupted as the driver suddenly called out to the team of horses to stop. She grabbed on to the door, enabling her to stay seated, while the coach slowed to a jarring, erratic stop. Pulling the curtain aside, she started to look out to see what had caused the 'whip' to stop — the breeze happened to be blowing toward her side of the coach — and she was immediately greeted by a dust cloud that swirled right into her face!

She sputtered, blew a puff of air through her lips to keep from getting a mouthful of grit, and quickly closed the window covering. The hasty effort did little to reduce the lingering powder-fine haze within the passenger cabin.

'Hey, Scotty!' she heard the stage jockey call out. 'What'n hell are you doing out here in the middle of buzzard and scorpion country?'

'Thanks for stopping, Mike,' a second voice reached her ears. 'Crossed trails with a couple Apache yesterday morning and they killed my horse. I've been afoot since then.'

'Them renegades ain't still around, are they?' The driver's voice revealed his concern.

'Not those two anyhow. They thought I was hit and came in a little too close.

9

You won't cross their trail unless you happen to visit the Great Spirit in the sky.'

'I reckon God and the Great Spirit are One and the same, Scotty, but I intend to put off that visit as long as possible.'

'Can I catch a ride with you?' the newcomer asked.

'Toss your rig and long gun up here to Bud. We'll tend to them for you.'

'How-do, Bud.' Scotty's voice sounded mellow and smooth, as he greeted the guard. 'You're new, aren't you?'

'Second trip,' the guard replied. 'I wanted to check out Little Babylon for myself. It's sure enough something a man doesn't see very often.'

The driver guffawed. 'Don't see anything like it anywhere else is more like it . . . though there might be the same kind of bandit stronghold across the border in the badlands of Mexico.'

Now that most of the dust had settled, Amy took another peek out the window. She could see a man approach the stage, saddle slung over one shoulder and a rifle in his free hand. Something about him caused an inner stir of excitement. Rugged and capable in appearance, he was attired in a cotton shirt — rolled up at the sleeves — wearing Kentucky jeans, aged and weathered riding boots and a moderately worn, wide-rimmed, crease-crowned hat. Other than the saddle and rifle, he carried a gun on one hip and a skinning knife on the other.

She closed the curtain again, immediately speculating about the new arrival's occupation — expressman, hawker, lawman or sawyer — yet he could be a cow puncher, horse wrangler . . . perhaps even an outlaw. She quickly pushed the unconscious drunk to the floor of the coach, so that it would force the newcomer to sit next to or directly across from her. Then she dug out her handkerchief and removed some of the dust from her face and brow. She had the cloth put back away when the coach door opened.

'Ma'am?' the man greeted her, his face hidden partly by alkali dust, sweat and several days' growth of facial hair. His eyes were gray — not the ashen gray of a weathered pole on a corral fence, more the color of smoke from burning coal — and he immediately held her captive with his appreciative gaze. A beguiling smile belied his dominating perusal. 'I'd be obliged if you'd allow me to share the coach with you.'

Amy gawked momentarily — kicked herself mentally to get her thinking process working — and replied, 'Certainly.' With a tip of her head toward the drunk. 'Don't mind Banger Jones. I believe he's still sleeping off the good time he had last week.'

The man had barely time to climb aboard before the team lurched forward and they were quickly moving down the bumpy trail. He eased past her, pulling the door closed behind him. She noted he was a considerate man as he hoisted Jones up on to the seat opposite Amy and sat next to the other coach window, leaving a respectful amount of space between them on the cushion.

'Maybe Mr Jones has the right idea about coach travel,' he said, opening the conversation. 'It's a long, dry haul to Little Babylon.'

'The driver said we would have to travel all night to get there,' she replied.

He took a moment to flex his rather wide shoulders — obviously stiff from carrying his saddle — and nodded. 'No way stations out here.'

'Did I hear you say something about Indians being nearby?'

'About the only people you find in this part of the territory are renegade Indians, rustlers, bandits and desperadoes from Wanted posters.' He gave her an inquisitive look. 'Little Babylon is the lone niche of civilization on the stage route between here and Santa Fe.'

'I've heard it is a lawless stronghold, full of killers and thieves.'

'That's what they say, although I've never been there myself.'

She frowned. 'But I heard you address the driver. I thought you must reside somewhere nearby.'

'Mike used to drive the Raton to Pueblo run a year or two back. I rode with him a number of times — atop the coach to keep him company on more than one occasion.'

They exchanged small talk for the next few minutes. Amy discovered Scotty was candid and real, a what-you-see-is-what-you-get kind of person. They discussed their home towns, growing up and their families. He seemed honest and trustworthy, so much so that she soon felt quite comfortable around him.

'Are you intending to disembark at the bandit den or are you going on to Santa Fe?' she asked, turning to the present situation.

'I figure to stick around Little Babylon for a spell.'

She raised a questioning eyebrow. 'And why are you going to visit such a wild town? You're not on the run from the law?'

He showed an amusement at her apprehension. 'No, I've got some business there.' Then pinning her with a cool, invasive gaze, 'What about you? You come from a large, civilized city, where you had family and friends. You can't be serious about staying at such a wild and untamed place on your own?'

'It's research relating to my profession — I'm a writer,' she informed him with pride.

'A writer?' he repeated, displaying both admiration and curiosity.

'Perhaps you've seen one of my books?' She opened her satchel, pulled out a dime novel and handed it to him.

'*Tornado Tess and the Massacre at River Bend*,' he read the title, '*As told by A.J. Cole*.' He looked up from the paperback book. 'You're A.J. Cole?'

'Yes, Amanda Jane Cole.'

'I saw some of these on a shelf at a store one time . . . though not this one in particular. They all had titles with wild-sounding names for women folk — *Mountain Millie and the Rustlers*,

River Kate and the Pirates, that sort of stuff.'

'Women like to read adventurous stories too.' She defended her chosen field. 'And many men also buy this kind of book.'

'So, Tornado Tess . . . you are writing about yourself?'

'It's all fiction — make-believe,' she scoffed at the notion. 'But my heroine is a detective. She actually solves crimes, rather than besting villains with her fighting skill or the use of guns.'

'I heard that Alan Pinkerton has a woman or two on his payroll,' the man said. 'Mostly for railroad work, catching crooked conductors or the like.'

'Yes, well my Tess does much more than report cheaters or the skimming of monies on railroad cars. She solves genuine crimes — murder, theft, arson — like a man might do.'

'Sounds interesting,' he said, opening the book. He flipped through the pages and stopped to read a passage aloud. '*His touch was the warmth of the sun* on an early spring morning, as he caressed her cheek with a gentle hand. *Tess had never imagined that a man so virile and strong could demonstrate such tenderness. Her good sense told her to forget Trapper Joe, but her heart refused to listen. She was lost to . . . '*

Amy snatched the book from his hand. 'You don't have to read it to me, Mr Scotty,' she said, suffering a flush of embarrassment at his chosen passage. 'I wrote it.'

'Actually, my name is Whitney Scott,' he said, overlooking her abrupt retrieval of her book, 'not Scotty.'

'Oh, I heard the driver call you by the name.'

'Yes, it's a nickname he gave me.'

'What do your friends call you?'

'Either Whitney or Scott . . . sometimes bonehead or dummy . . . depends on the friend.'

She laughed. 'My friends call me Amy, rather than Amanda.' With rashness she didn't often display she went on, 'And, as we will be traveling together all night, I should like for you to call me Amy as well.'

'I'd consider that an honor,' he said, exhibiting an unaffected smile. 'I haven't called a girl by her first name since my sister left home.'

'You can't be serious!'

'Well, I'm referring to a proper lady, such as yourself,' he explained. 'Most of the gals I come across are married or working at dance halls and saloons. There isn't an abundance of single, genteel women this side of the Colorado-New Mexico border.'

'I don't think you mentioned what line of work you were in.'

'Up until a couple weeks ago, I used to be a rancher.'

'Used to be?'

'I still own the place ... a horse ranch this side of Raton,' he replied. 'We ran about two hundred head of horses.'

'Sounds like a big place.'

'It was — until we got hit by a band of rustlers. They stole the entire herd and killed my younger brother, along with a couple hired hands and the woman who cooked for us. I never did find our third hired man. He was out watching the herd, so his body is probably out in the hills somewhere.'

'How dreadful!' she exclaimed. 'All this time together and you never said a word about such a horrible tragedy.'

He sobered. 'Yeah, well that's the business I was talking about.'

'You think the killers are holed up in Little Babylon?'

'I've been on their trail for some time now,' he answered. 'Little Babylon is my next stop. Plus, I'll have to pick me up another horse.'

'How many men are you chasing?'

'I'm not sure — three brothers and a gunhand or two.'

Amy was aghast. 'And you're all alone?'

'Not much law in New Mexico Territory, except in a few of the bigger towns. I'm friends with the US marshal who lives in Colorado Springs. I sent him a wire to tell him what had happened and he gave me the go-ahead, kind of like an unofficial deputy.'

'Why didn't you request to be deputized yourself?'

'Because I didn't want to worry about rules,' the man answered bluntly, a cool frost entering his eyes. 'If I catch up to two or three men at once, I'm not going to ask them to surrender politely and get myself shot full of holes. I'll worry about having them arrested after I have them hogtied, locked in a cell or laid out in wooden boxes.'

The idea of vigilante justice should have shocked a city girl, but Amy understood his logic. 'That makes sense.'

Her approval surprised him. 'You approve of a man taking the law into his own hands?'

'As you stated, there is no law out here. I don't see there are any other options.'

He let the matter drop. 'Why is a writer of make-believe adventures going to Little Babylon? It's no place for a decent woman.'

'I too am searching for someone,' she replied, intoning a bit of self-righteousness into her voice. 'Someone who is seeking my help.'

Puzzlement entered his expression at once. 'I thought you said Tess wasn't real?'

Amy had not told anyone of her quest, not even her father when he objected to her leaving home. But her fear of the unknown had mounted with each passing mile. She realized she might need an ally, in case she wound up in an awkward or dangerous situation.

'A reader of my books wrote and asked for my help,' she confided after a moment. 'I can't ignore the plea to save an innocent man's life.'

'Why would a person write to you, rather than contacting a lawyer or the US marshal?'

Impulsively, she removed the worn letter from her purse. The road had smoothed out for the present, so she was able to unfold it and hold it where Whitney could see it. He read aloud.

Dear A. J. Cole,
I can't help writing to tell you how much I enjoy your books. My favorite title is The Framed Man. I can see you care for the characters and I like how when someone looks guilty, often The Reverse Is True. We need writers like you who don't doctor facts to fit the crimes. Please don't stop writing.

> *Sincerely,*
> *A Fan.*

Whitney stared at the bottom of the page, where several numbers were listed, each separated by a dash mark. 'What are the numbers for?'

'In the book, *Tornado Tess and the Framed Man*, Tess gets a message from a man in prison. He's certain someone will read his letter before mailing it, so he uses a numbered code so he can express his innocence. Each number matches to a word in the letter.'

Whitney took a moment to look at the page and shook his head. 'Let's see, three would be the first number; twelve is the second . . . the third . . . ' He studied the message. 'The numbers don't make any sense. It starts out with *help your need?*'

'Exactly what I thought until I reread the wording. See how she capitalized the words *The Reverse Is True?*' At his nod, she clarified, 'If you put the numbers at the bottom of the page in reverse order, it reads: *The framed man is a doctor. I need your help.*'

'Clever,' he replied. 'And you called the writer *she?*'

'Yes, whoever wrote this is a woman. You can tell by the delicate hand.'

He glanced over the page again. 'There's no name and the only address is Little Babylon.'

Amy gave her head a nod. 'Yes, but I doubt there is more than one doctor in such a place. I'm sure either he or whoever wrote this will find a way to contact me.'

Whitney grunted a snort of contempt. 'You're wading into quicksand while wearing a blindfold, lady. Little Babylon isn't a town, it's a bandit fortress. There are armed guards at the gates and even the army would hesitate about trying to take the place by force.'

'You said you had never been there?'

'I haven't, but I did some checking before I decided to enter the place to search for the men who killed my brother. Story goes, a man called Huntley started a trading post, added a saloon and boarding house and continued to build. He put up a wall around the entire town to defend against Indian attacks. He has twenty armed men working for him and owns everything inside the walls.'

'I thought it was a bandit stronghold,' she said. 'How does one man control a bunch of killers and thieves?'

'He offers security and protection, along with hard liquor, women, gambling, board and room — one fellow told me he even invites theater groups to perform there. The man has made himself king and rules with an iron hand.'

'If the killers you seek are safe inside his fortress, how do you intend to get at them?'

'My first chore is to find them.'

Amy's brain was racing. 'Maybe I could help you in your quest?' she offered. 'No one will suspect me of working undercover for you, and you could help me with my problem.'

'I don't know how to go about proving someone was framed.'

'I do.'

His eyebrows lifted with incredulity. 'You're telling me you're an actual detective?'

'Not exactly, but I've read the *Police Gazette* for years along with everything ever written about detective work. Once I meet the doctor, and discover the story behind his being wrongfully accused, I'll figure out a way to determine the guilty party and clear his name.'

Whitney laughed. 'Got to give you credit for brass, ma'am. You surely don't lack for confidence.'

'It's why I ventured out to the untamed West, to live an adventure and put realism in my books. I'm not afraid to stick out my neck a bit.'

He shook his head. 'Miss Cole, you obviously have courage, but the town ahead is likely a nest of vermin, the sludge of the earth, and it caters to some of the worst men in the country. A few of those characters will have no conscience about treating you the same as they would the lowest tramp or a wandering bum. Being a lady doesn't make a difference to a hardened killer.'

'I appreciate your concern, Mr Scott,' she introduced a coolness to her voice, 'but I am going to visit Little Babylon and conduct my interviews. Even if I can't find a way to help this innocent man, I can rise above the competition in my field by instilling authentic pragmatism into my stories. And, if I should succeed, I can state my account is based on facts. It will elevate my stories to a new level.'

'You won't sell a single story if you

end up dead or working in a saloon as a prisoner for the next dozen years.'

Amy almost fired back about how she could take care of herself, but she resisted the urge. A new plan of attack entered her head. With a sly upward curl of her lips she said, 'All the more reason we should work together.'

'Ma'am, I couldn't risk involving you.'

'Then tell me your plan, Scotty,' she challenged, purposely using his nickname. 'How are you going to find those ruthless murderers and bring them to justice? Are you going to wade in with guns blazing and get a dozen people killed? Or do you intend to sneak about under the cover of darkness and execute them one at a time?'

'I'll worry about how to deal with them once I locate them.'

'What if I could help you do that without anyone knowing who you are? Wouldn't that be a big help?' She hurried to add, 'And you could help me at the same time.'

'Help you?'

'I'm not as capable in a fight as Tornado Tess. She saved a man from India in her first book and learned Varma Kalai, a secret form of self-defense.'

'Varma — who?' Whitney asked.

'Varma Kalai is a secret form of fighting intended for self-defense. It teaches the vital pressure points in the human body and how to stop an attacker without doing any permanent damage.' She sighed, 'Unfortunately, I never actually studied the craft. The man I talked to said I would have to travel to India and it takes a student ten to fifteen years to learn all of a master teacher's secrets.'

'Sounds like we could both use Tess on our side.'

Amy laughed, but remained serious about her plan. 'If you're interested, I have an idea that will serve both of our purposes.'

'It's a long way to Little Babylon,' he said. 'You talk, I'll listen.'

2

J.D. Huntley sipped his medicine-tea concoction and watched Belva counting the receipts from last night. He trusted her — well, as much as he trusted anyone — but he was always present to look over her final totals before sticking the money in his safe.

'Slow night,' Belva observed.

'No theater group this week,' Huntley said. 'We have a Shakespeare troupe due in on Tuesday. That ought to add to our tally.'

'I was approached by a couple of men over at the pharmacy who asked about getting a loan or writing an IOU while in town.'

'What did you tell them?'

She smiled, 'That Helen Waite was in charge of giving credit.'

Huntley laughed. 'I get it — if you want to borrow money, go to *hell and wait*.'

'However, the cash balance of some of your regulars has gone down steadily in recent weeks. And we don't seem to have as many new arrivals lately.'

'I fear the law is beefing up along the borders, now most of the Indian problems have been settled. With the Apache, Navajo and Comanche mostly confined to reservations, there are concerns about putting an end to some of the lawlessness of this vast territory. It is fortunate for us that there are but a few settlements nearby of any size. The cattle barons make their own laws and we don't infringe on their land or challenge their authority.'

'The banks in both Colorado Springs and Santa Fe honored all of the bank notes we sent on our last trip. I have another batch prepared for the next time you want to send out Cyrus or Nickel.'

'I do so enjoy your formal training, from back when you were working for a bank,' Huntley said. 'You are organized and keep records better than anyone I ever had working for me.'

'You did promise to allow us our freedom to leave whenever we asked,' she reminded him. 'Ralph and I said we would work for you, but not unconditionally.'

'Yes, yes, I remember, Belva. A deal is a deal, I won't renege on our agreement.'

'And you'll pay us in full if and when we decide to leave?'

'Certainly,' he was again agreeable. 'I presume you are keeping track of what I owe you?'

'Between my chores here, Ralph's work as town doctor and the running of the pharmacy, we agreed upon eighty dollars a month, over our room and board,' she recounted. 'After our withdrawals, you owe us a little over two hundred dollars.' She quickly added, 'Everything is written down and itemized for you in the accounts payable ledger.'

He displayed an admiring smile at her proficiency. 'As I was saying, you are worth every penny, my dear lady.'

Belva was matronly, well past thirty, with gray streaks in her otherwise faded blond hair. A bit weighty, she was still comely and had a pleasing personality. He regarded her like he would have an older sister or maiden aunt. While she spent most of her day working at the town pharmacy, she came in each morning to count and enter his receipts. Not only did she have a good head for figures, but her penmanship was neat and legible and she kept all of the revenue journals concise and up to date. It had been a stroke of luck having her arrive with the doctor.

The door opened and Bruno stuck his head into the room. 'Boss, stage just come in. Nickel says you ought to take a look. He's downstairs.'

Belva pushed back from the table. 'The books are done,' she said. 'I'm going to get something to eat.'

'Of course,' Huntley said. 'I'll see you tomorrow.'

Belva left the room as he swallowed

the last of his tea and set down the empty cup. He took a few moments to stick everything in the huge 1,000lb safe and closed the door. With a spin of the dial, he hurried out of the back room and went to see what Nickel thought was so important.

As was his habit, Bruno waited for him. He followed along wordlessly, constantly keeping watch over his boss. A big man, he never asked questions and did as he was told. Huntley had never uncovered the reason behind him killing a man with his bare hands. However, after he secured the man's freedom, Bruno had become his trusted watchdog. Occasionally, he was more than a bodyguard . . . but that was something Huntley didn't enjoy thinking about.

Nickel was a completely different breed of employee. He dressed in expensive suits, silk shirts, glossy-shined boots and wore twenty-dollar hats. He hired out his twin Colts and maintained an unquestioning loyalty, but he worked strictly for cash money and demanded enough free time to spend it. Huntley granted him a day off each week and allowed Nickel to use it as he wished. Sometimes the man took the day during the week, though he would often save up two or three days and take them all at once. He was one of the two men Huntley trusted to cash in the banknotes he honored and return with the money.

'I 'spect you'll want to have a look at what arrived on the stage, boss.' Nickel showed a salacious grin. 'This one's a real beaut.'

Huntley crossed over to stand at Nickel's side. The man uttered a satisfied grunt and tipped his head toward a fashionable lady on the walk. She was brushing dust from her russet-colored traveling outfit while a seasoned and capable-looking gent collected her luggage. Even from that distance Huntley could see the girl was something special.

'What do we know about her?'

'I was across the street when the stage pulled up. She went in and got a room at the hotel while the whip was delivering the mail bag. I checked with Henry, but the gal didn't say much, other than that she is staying in town for a few days.'

'And the man, the one helping with her things?'

'I heard the driver call him Scotty — his saddle is topside with the luggage.'

'Then he isn't with the young lady,' Huntley mused. 'I can't believe she would come here alone and unescorted.'

'That's the odd part, boss — the gal signed for two rooms. It appears the gent is acting the part of her bodyguard.'

'Yet he arrives with his saddle?' Huntley harrumphed his bewilderment at the idea. 'Something doesn't make sense.'

'Few horses can keep up with the stage. They change teams every day and the last leg is an all-nighter into town.'

'You're right, Nickel, his horse might

have given out . . . or he left him at one of the way stations. However, it's still curious as to why he would bring along his saddle, rather than travel as an ordinary escort.'

'Want me to do some checking about him or the gal for you?'

'We'll wait until the young lady is settled in,' Huntley told him. 'Wouldn't hurt to see what you can find out about the stranger.'

'From the cut of his outfit he looks as if he's done some hard traveling,' Nickel observed. 'Looks more like someone on the run from the law than a bodyguard.'

'Most men who come here are wanted for something,' Huntley agreed. 'The question is what's his relationship with the girl?'

'I'll nose around and get back to you, boss.'

Huntley managed a nod to show he was satisfied with the plan, while he could not tear his eyes away from the scarlet-haired beauty. Being the ruler of a small kingdom was a thankless and all-consuming job. How much better life would be if he had a beautiful queen at his side!

★　★　★

Whitney carried the young lady's things into her room and set them down. He quickly moved over and peered from behind the curtain, watching the street.

'That jasper with a badge, the one who was snooping around at the hotel when we arrived, is now talking to Mike,' he told Amy. 'I'd wager one or both of us are the subject of the conversation.'

'It's to be expected,' she replied. 'After all, this is a town of miscreants and desperadoes. Whatever form of law enforcement they use, I would surmise they keep a close eye on people who come and go.'

'If that's the case, it will be no secret that I got on the stage twenty miles down the trail. Your idea about my being your bodyguard is not going to hold much water.'

'I've worked out the details,' she stated with confidence. At his curious glance, she explained, 'The bodyguard I started out with turned out to be a weak-kneed milksop so I dismissed him. I hired you on the spot when we met, so I wouldn't have to enter such an unsavory and barbarous town with no protection.'

He grinned. 'You have the mind of a storyteller, that's a fact.'

'Would you ask about a bath for me?' she remained businesslike. 'I want to clean up and put on fresh clothes before I make a formal appearance on the street.'

'Yes, ma'am,' Whitney answered. 'The sign behind the counter said something about a New York bath being available . . . whatever that is.'

'I thought you were going to call me Amy?'

'Got to play the role,' he said. 'My being your hired help, it would not be proper to address you by your first name.'

'You're right,' she replied. 'However, I will call you Scotty. It will hide your identity and,' displaying a mischievous simper, 'being your employer, it's my prerogative.'

'Yeah . . . my mother used that *prerogative* word a lot with my father.'

She laughed at the comment, but displayed a serious mien, 'Your parents are both gone now?'

'Dad when I was about sixteen and Mom two years later. I kind of raised my younger brother after that.'

She returned to business. 'I didn't notice when I signed the register for the two of us, where is your room?'

'Down the hall two doors,' he replied. 'I need to pick up a few things . . . some new clothes, shaving stuff and such. Had to leave everything behind but my saddle and rifle, so I don't even have a change of socks.'

Amy took out her timepiece and looked at it. 'After I take the bath, I'm going to try and get a couple hours' sleep. I didn't get much rest on the stage last night.'

'Whatever you say, ma'am . . . you're the detective.'

She smiled at his statement and he forgot about why he had come to such a lawless part of the world. He mentally kicked himself and forced his feet to move.

'I'll put my gun and saddle in my room and order up that bath for you,' he said, making his exit.

After Whitney had brought up his things, he left them in the room and went back outside to speak to Mike. He discovered the driver had sent Bud to the livery end of town to put up the team and coach.

'So you spend the day, get some sleep tonight and head back tomorrow morning?' he asked Mike.

'Yeah, I hate the hard pull coming here,' he replied. 'Wish to hell they would set up another station half way between here and Alkali Springs. Dangerous and slow to travel at night, but no way we're going to stop out in the badlands and spend the night without shelter or protection.'

'Can I pay you something for the ride?'

Mike waved his hand in a dismissive gesture. 'You was afoot, Scotty. Besides, I ain't forgot how you helped me the night we lost a wheel over near Stormy Gulch.' He laughed. 'By jingo, that was a chore in the pouring rain.'

'I never waded in so much mud in all my life, that's a fact.'

'I'd have still been stuck in that muck hole if you hadn't been on the coach. No sir,' he snorted, 'you don't owe me one damn thing.'

'Thanks, Mike.'

He might have turned to walk away, but the driver took a step closer and spoke in a hushed voice. 'Some flinty-eyed son was asking about you and the gal,' he informed Whitney. 'I didn't give him much about you, only that the Apache had kilt your horse. As for the lady, I know she's a scribe or writer, something like that. Anyways, that's all I told him.'

'Much obliged, Mike. There isn't much more to tell, other than the lady hired me to look out for her while we're in town.'

'That could be a big job, Scotty. I don't rightly know the name of the man who was asking the questions, but he's one of the regulators who work for J.D. Huntley, the man who runs this here town.'

'Regulators?'

'They do the job of marshal . . . along with anything else the big honcho wants.'

'I heard a little about Huntley from a couple wranglers we hired last year.'

'Well, if them fellows said anything about him being a kind or gentle soul, they got him mixed up with someone else. He rules with a firm hand and has the regulators to back his play.'

Whitney shook the driver's hand. 'Be seeing you, Mike — maybe next trip.'

The man stepped to the side and bobbed his head. 'Shore 'nuff. You keep your eyes open and gun handy, Scotty.

If I don't see you before we leave in the morning, I'll be back this way in a week.'

Whitney entered the boarding house again and stopped at the desk. An elderly gent was making entries in a book, but paused to look up. 'Yes, Scotty?'

The use of his nickname caused Whitney to pause. 'Do I know you, old-timer?'

He smiled. 'The lassie put your name on the register,' he explained. 'No first or last name, only Scotty.'

'Yeah, I prefer to protect the family name . . . kind of an embarrassment for them at times, if you know what I mean.'

'I understand completely,' he answered back. 'I've had no less than a dozen Smiths rent a room in the past month. Not very original, some of these criminal sorts.'

'The lady would like a bath — your sign says New York style? What kind of bath is that?'

'We've a luxury spa in the back,

complete with a marble tub — indoor plumbed, direct from a water tank, with a coal-fired heater for warming the water. It includes scented bathing oils and imported shampoo for the ladies.' He grinned, 'Nothing but first rate here at Huntley's Hotel.'

'Sounds impressive,' Whitney replied. 'Didn't know there was anything so fancy this side of Denver.'

'Cost a small fortune to get the tub and heater shipped out here and installed, but Huntley wanted the best.'

Whitney drew his brows into a frown. 'What about privacy? My employer is a fine-looking lady and I'd take serious exception to anyone spying or intruding on her.'

'There's a vent for air flow, but no windows, and a bolt-lock is on the inside of the door. She'll be perfectly safe. You have my personal promise, no one is going to disturb her during her bath.'

'About the room rent . . . ?'

'Miss Cole paid for both rooms

44

— twenty dollars. The bath is another five, but I'll trust her to pay before she leaves.'

'Twenty dollars for the rooms?'

'Ten dollars each room, each night,' he explained. 'This is a premier establishment. The lower-class clientele choose the cheaper rooms at the Bunk House, just down the street.'

'Never really thought about an outlaw stronghold catering to the wealthy.'

The man smiled, 'Mr Huntley is in business to make money. Those who can afford it stay here, but everyone pays their own way. You'll find no beggars, drummers or tin-horn gamblers in this town.'

'Just killers and thieves.'

The clerk laughed, 'Yes, but only those with money.'

'I understand,' Whitney said. 'I'll tell the lady about the bath.'

'I'll go light the fire for her so the water can start to heat. It ought to be ready in a few minutes.'

'Much obliged, Mr . . . ?'

The old gent chuckled, '*Smith*, Henry Smith.'

Whitney grinned at the last name and turned for the stairs.

★　★　★

Amy felt spoiled and refreshed after the hot bath. Instead of a nap, she sat with a notebook in her hands, writing line after line, the words flowing with ease. This was great stuff! Meeting Whitney — Scotty, to protect his identity — and adding his quest to her own case had been inspirational.

She decided to call her counterpart hero Flash McCord. He was a fabulous dresser, with twin pearl-handled Colts and custom-made Colorado cutaway holsters. His suit and vest were coal-black, with a white silk shirt, polished boots, and a black, thirty-dollar Stetson, set off by an inch-wide, plated-silver hat band. Even his neckerchief was black, though he carried a white silk handkerchief for lending to a lady.

He was the ultimate gentleman, defending the honor of any man, woman or child, able to stand against a dozen men without the slightest hint of fear. For his actual looks and build, she chose to stick with Whitney, because . . . well, because he looked like a hero.

She paused to read what she had written and was very pleased. This would be a story to be proud of, a book with grit and reality and truth. No pretense about fictional victims or a band of imaginary villains. This was beyond fantasy, beyond a writer's imagination — it was real! It was living a story, being a part —

A sudden hammering nearly broke down her door!

'You in there!' a guttural voice grated. 'Open up! We come to get you!'

She dropped her writing materials and scooted off the bed. Her heart thundered in her ears and a naked fear invaded her chest. What was going on?

The banging came again, louder this time. She covered her mouth with her hand to prevent screaming in fright. The entire room rattled and shook from the force of the man's fists. She feared the flimsy lock would not hold and the door would fly off of its hinges. Who was in the hallway and why did they want her?

* * *

Whitney had spent a couple hours looking over the town and then picked up a shirt and trousers, along with the other things he would be needing. Once back at his room, he had used a pan of water to wash and shave, before changing into his new clothes. He was staring in the mirror, thinking he ought to get a haircut when he heard banging and shouting down the hall.

'Open up, yuh little storytelling vixen!' a man's voice rang out. 'You're gonna come and have a drink with us!'

'Yeah, by jingo!' another man joined

in. 'We'll show you some of the stuff you don't read in books!'

Grabbing up his gun-belt, Whitney strapped it on hurriedly and stepped out into the corridor. Two scruffy-looking men were in front of Amy's door. Both were lanky gents with the hard look of troublemakers. He started in their direction and both men whirled to face him. It didn't take a lot of contemplating to know the two had been expecting him to intervene.

'Howdy, boys,' Whitney greeted the pair with a natural smile, quickly closing the distance. He knew most men wouldn't go for their gun when confronted toe to toe. His rapid approach not only blocked the notion of gunplay, it also put them at a disadvantage because they were stand-ing at the head of the stairs. 'You looking for someone?'

'What's it to you, stranger?' the taller of the two spoke up snidely. 'It's supposed to be the gal who does the writing!'

Whitney laughed to keep the men off guard. 'Right you are, friend. However the lady staying in this room is resting up from a week-long stagecoach ride. How about you come back later?'

'You kin butt outa' this,' the one warned, 'else Ike and me will take you apart like a toy puzzle.'

'Skeet is telling it straight,' the other agreed. 'We come to show the gal around and you'd be right smart to stay out of this.'

Whitney continued to show a good-natured smile. He held up both hands, palms outward as if wanting no part of any trouble. 'Sure thing, fellas. I was only making sure you had the right room. The lady is nothing special to me.'

'Then you best skedaddle, sonny boy,' Ike sneered, 'whilst we are still feeling generous.'

With his hands already raised, Whitney suddenly charged into the two men and shoved them backward. Ike missed the top step and grabbed hold of Skeet, who also lost his balance. Both of them went crashing down the stairs, tumbling and rolling, with arms and legs tangled, cursing with every bounce.

Whitney followed after them, pushing them along with his boot, until they were all the way to the bottom step. He quickly moved in and took both of their guns before they could get free of one another.

Skeet sat up and grabbed his left wrist, having twisted it during the fall. A drop of blood seeped from a cut lip on Ike's lip, as he had hit his mouth on the railing on his way down. Both were slow to get up, baring their teeth and glowering at Whitney.

'Sorry about the shove, boys,' he spoke in a calm voice, 'but I lied to you about the gal upstairs meaning nothing to me. She's under my protection.'

'You took advantage pushing us like you done!' Ike complained.

'I didn't want any trouble.'

'Trouble, says you,' Skeet growled. 'You kick us down the stairs like a couple stray dogs and you ain't looking for trouble?'

'I don't know who sent you,' Whitney said easily, 'but you can tell him the lady will decide who she will talk to and when.' He took a moment to empty the guns of both men and then passed the pistols to them.

'This ain't over,' Ike warned.

'Look, fellas,' Whitney said easily, 'I'm just doing what I've been paid to do . . . same as you. I only knocked you down the stairs so I wouldn't have to kill you both.'

'Mighty tall talking, friend,' Skeet growled. 'What makes you think you could take both of us?'

'At less than ten feet? Inside a closed-in hallway?' Whitney shook his head. 'Boys, you have to know — had it come to gun play — we would have all three ended up shot to pieces.' As the pair exchanged looks, he added, 'I don't know about you, but I'm not getting paid enough to get killed.'

The two men, both on their feet now,

finally appeared to relax.

'Reckon you got a point,' Skeet admitted. 'We was supposed to have some fun with the book-writing lady.'

'Yeah, we weren't looking for a killing fight.'

'I'm glad to hear it,' Whitney said. 'I'd as soon not get shot full of holes myself. Thing is, I'm taking the lady's money to see to her safety. You see how it is?'

Ike glowered at him. 'It seems we ought to bust you up a little for treating us like you done.'

'How about we settle this in a more peaceable manner, boys?' Whitney offered, digging out a couple coins. 'Here, you two can go have a few drinks on me.'

The two exchanged looks and both seemed satisfied that the ruckus was over. Ike took the offered money while Whitney regarded the other man with a look of concern. 'Your wrist OK?' he asked Skeet. 'Sure didn't intend to break any bones.'

'I twisted it a might, but it's all right,'

Skeet told him, flexing the wrist as proof. 'I don't bounce as good as when I was younger.'

Whitney laughed. 'I know what you mean. Last time I got thrown from a horse I didn't walk right for a week.'

The two men said so long, rotated about and walked toward the exit. Smith was at the counter and had taken a shotgun from beneath the counter. He put the weapon away, seeing the trouble had passed.

'Is it over?' a familiar voice asked from the top of the stairs.

Whitney looked up at the most beautiful creature he'd ever seen. Her hair was still damp, but had been brushed out; she wore a cornflower-colored chiffon dress with lace and ruffles; yet she hadn't bothered to put on her shoes. Her face was clear of dust and without rouge, allowing him to see she had a complexion as smooth as polished ivory.

'I think God best take inventory,' Whitney praised. 'One of His angels has sure enough escaped from heaven.'

Instead of speaking, Amy's mouth opened . . . then closed abruptly, and she whirled about to rush back to her room.

What the Sam Hill is that all about? Whitney wondered.

'Figured you was in for a fight,' Henry Smith spoke up, having walked over to stand at Whitney's side. 'Ike and Skeet can make a nuisance of themselves sometimes.'

'I suspect they were on a mission — came to test me — if I read it right.'

'They might have only wanted to have a gander at the lady. She's quite a looker and word travels fast in this town.' He shrugged his bony shoulders. 'But, you're right, they were probably testing you to see if you were an actual bodyguard. A stranger enters town with only a saddle and rifle — could mean a lot of different things.'

Whitney shrugged. 'Those boys only had to ask. A couple Indians killed my horse. I met the lady on the stage and she offered me a job . . . nothing all that secretive about anything.'

Henry eyed him for a long moment, as if gaging his truthfulness. 'I reckon you proved your point to the brainless twosome. They know you ain't the kind who will run.'

Whitney chuckled. 'Every man will run — sic an angry bear on him and watch.'

'Yep, but a smart man knows he can't outrun a bear — he has to out-think it.'

'You getting philosophical on me are you, Henry?'

'I'm not sure what that word even means, so I reckon you can just jot it down as advice.'

'Why are you out in the middle of nowhere, running a boarding house for a man like Huntley?'

'Like most everyone else who actually lives here, I made a mistake one time and have been paying for it ever since. Sometimes I think I'd have been better off to stay and face my problems.'

'Considering the town you chose to hide in, I'd say you made the wrong choice.'

'I'll maybe leave here one day,' Henry said. 'Till then, I'll bide my time and try to stay out of trouble.'

'I wish you luck.'

'Don't go wishing away something you can't have too much of around here.'

'One question, Henry, was the shotgun meant for me or the two nitwits?'

He grinned. 'I don't allow no one to harass my guests . . . but a blast with both barrels would have likely splattered all three of you.'

'Fine, just so I know I don't owe you any thanks.'

Henry laughed and returned to the counter. Whitney was curious about Amy's odd reaction but decided to find a barber. Wearing new clothes didn't mean much if a man looked like a shaggy dog from the neck up.

3

Amy held up her hand — it trembled uncontrollably — and she was shivering, as if standing next to a drafty window. With an outside temperature in the mid-eighties, there was no reason for a physical chill. It dawned on her what that meant.

Hearing the two men bang on her door, she had been afraid . . . really afraid. She had traveled through towns of all sizes and had even witnessed a fight or two. However, she had never been accosted or molested in her life. Her father and two older brothers had protected her growing up, sometimes to the extent of frightening away potential suitors. But today, with two rowdy men demanding she go with them . . .

She blocked the dread, thankful Whitney had come to her aid. When the talking became a ruckus, she had peeked out into the hallway in time to see him booting the two men down the stairs. He had stood up for her like a hero from one of her books and sent the troublemakers on their way.

But what would I have done if Whitney had not been here?

The stark realization that she was beyond the law and civilization crashed down upon her world like a giant meteor. *I must be out of my mind!*

Her zeal for writing had caused her to come to this forbidden land and risk her very life. She had allowed the legend of Tornado Tess to consume her good sense. She wasn't the character in her book; she had no special skills in self-defense. She had only met the man from India at a party and learned of the secret society of Varma Kalai via her charm. Was a trace of realism worth getting someone killed? What if the two men had tried to shoot it out with Whitney? He could have been killed . . . or have had to kill one or both of those men in her defense.

She hated even to allow the notion into her head. Befittingly, she said a silent prayer of thanks for the capable rancher. It had been very fortunate having him board the stage and then agree to pretend he was her bodyguard. Presently, he offered the only glimmer of security for her while she was in such a lawless town.

Returning to her notebook, she decided the best way to handle this measure of trepidation was to scribble it down on paper. Of course, it would be necessary to embellish the action a bit and Tess would have to be more than a spectator. After all, she wrote fiction. She would use the three characters and let Tess jump in and save Flash McCord from an ambush. That ought to make the story more interesting for her readers!

★　★　★

The man waiting for Whitney when he left the barbershop was the same one he had seen asking Mike questions. He gave him no sign of recognition, prepared to walk past him . . . until the gent moved nonchalantly into Whitney's path.

'You Scotty?' he asked, although he obviously knew the answer.

'Yeah,' he replied. 'Who are you?'

'Nickel Eton,' he announced. Then tapping the badge on his chest, 'I work for J.D. Huntley. I'm a regulator — kind of a town marshal.'

'Huntley, he's the guy who started this bandit stronghold, isn't he?'

Nickel ignored the question. 'Rumor has it you knocked around a couple of locals a few minutes ago.'

Whitney grinned, 'You say locals or locos?'

Nickel's stern expression lifted to amusement. 'Those two do tend to be inept at times.'

'And you're what, an ex-gunman?'

'Actually, I'm a preacher's son . . . gone bad, Scotty,' he answered candidly. He patted the cream-colored handles on his pair of pistols. 'Being educated in the righteous path isn't always enough. I chose to look beyond my father's teachings and learn the truth of life on my own.'

'You find what you were looking for?'

Nickel laughed without mirth. 'What I found was my name on a Wanted poster. Seems I was a little too handy with a gun and lacked the good sense about when to use it.'

'That's happened to more than a few men.'

'How about you?' He was instantly serious again. 'When a man goes by a nickname, rather than formal title, it means he either hates his given name or he is on the run.'

'I suppose it's a little of both.'

He appeared satisfied with the answer. 'The boss would like to get together with the lady. I'm passing the word to you so there won't be any' — choosing his words carefully — 'friction between us.'

Whitney was agreeable. 'I'd as soon

stay on good terms with the town's law enforcement too. Plus Miss Cole is looking forward to meeting your boss. Name the time and place.'

'The invite is for her to join him for dinner over at Huntley's Refectory — next to the casino — at seven o'clock.'

'I'm sure the lady will be delighted.'

'I'll tell the boss to expect her' — he showed a smirk — 'just her.'

'I understand.'

He studied Whitney a moment longer, as if trying to place him into a category. 'Welcome to Little Babylon, Scotty.'

'Thanks, Nickel,' he answered back. 'It's already feeling like home.'

Nickel spun about and walked down the street. As Whitney watched him go, he let out the breath he'd been holding. The well-dressed man was lean and wiry, hand never far from his gun, with a smooth stride and a balance to his every move. Nickel looked very capable.

Dismissing the man from his thoughts, he went back to the hotel. When he reached the top of the stairs a man was leaving the room between his and Amy's. He had the look of a gambler, with gray above his ears and a natural squint from constant smoke of cigars and cigarettes. Whitney made a decision and stopped to talk to him.

★ ★ ★

As Amy sat in front of her mirror and attempted to put some curl in her hair, she heard voices in the hallway. She stopped primping, thinking one of them sounded like Whitney. When no one knocked at the door, she returned to using her hair brush. There was still the noise of someone opening and closing doors, but it went quiet after a few minutes so she dismissed her concern. It had likely been a new guest moving into or out of one of the nearby rooms.

Considering her next move, she had spied the pharmacy upon their arrival. And when she had signed the hotel register, Henry had told her a doctor ran the place — a woman also helped run the store. He didn't know much, or wasn't given to gossip, as he hadn't offered more information.

Amy stared at her own reflection, firming her resolve. She had been completely unnerved by the skirmish between Whitney and the two rowdies who came to fetch her. But she, along with her beloved Tess, had a renewed confidence, knowing their bodyguard was a very capable man. She vowed to continue her quest and also enquire about the three brothers who had stolen Whitney's herd of horses.

A tap at the door caused her heart to leap in her chest. She swallowed the rush of emotion and asked, 'Who is it?'

'It's me,' came an uncertain response, 'uh, Scotty. Miss Cole.'

Discarding the hairbrush, she hurried to open the door. She smiled at Whitney and his return smile caused an immediate warmth to engulf her. He was dressed in a black suit jacket and trousers, freshly groomed and shaved, holding his hat in his hands. However, his attire was not nearly so striking as the admiring expression which shone on his face.

'I only thought you looked like an angel before,' he said somewhat awkwardly, 'but seeing you now, I'd be willing to put money on the notion. Both smart and beautiful; that's some special combination.'

Amy had been flattered before, many times in fact, but never with more genuine appeal. His delivery actually made her feel extraordinary. It brightened the world and lifted her spirits at the same time.

'I'm not sure you should be so bold when you address your employer,' she teased.

'Can't fault a man for being truthful, Miss Cole.'

She gave him a quick once-over. 'You also clean up very nicely. I was curious as what you would look like without a week-old growth of beard and unshorn hair.'

'I have a meeting arranged for you.' He got down to business. 'Mr King-of-the-Fortress wishes to have you dine with him tonight. It's the eatery next to the casino with the peculiar name.'

'Yes, Huntley's Refectory . . . I saw it while the stage was unloading my things.'

'Seven o'clock,' he finished. 'His top gun was the man who delivered the invite.'

'I assume you were not as abrupt with him as the two ruffians who approached my door earlier?'

'He represents the law in town and was polite about the invite,' Whitney responded. 'And, seeing how this request was from J.D. Huntley, I figured you would want me to accept.'

'Yes, I'm anxious to meet him,' she said. 'He may hold the key to both of our problems.'

'You had best not be too obvious about using your detective skills. Huntley is one man we can't afford to cross.'

'I'll proceed with caution, Scotty. Can I impose on you to escort me to the restaurant at the proper hour?'

'Wouldn't have it otherwise,' he answered. 'It's best you don't go out on the street alone . . . not until you have Huntley's word that no one will bother you anyway.'

'I agree.' She offered up a tense smile. 'Guess this is it, it's really happening. I'm about to embark on a real mission to try and solve an actual case. It's' — she uttered a nervous laugh — 'it's both exciting and frightening.'

'*Two* cases,' he corrected, 'if you happen to discover the Polson boys are in town.'

'I won't forget.'

Whitney removed his timepiece and glanced at it. 'It's another hour before the meeting. I'll get myself something to eat and be back to walk you over.'

Amy took a deep breath to firm her resolve. 'Thank you, Scotty, I'll be ready.'

★ ★ ★

'I've got to be sure about this, Doc.' Huntley was gravely earnest. 'There can't be any chance of my having' — he disliked the usual terms so he finished — 'having any trouble.'

'You can't eat potassium bromide like it was candy,' Doctor Lyndell told him professionally. 'Even a slight excess could upset your system and make you queasy. The measured dose in your tea twice a day has worked up to now. So long as you don't get overexcited or tensed up, you should be fine.'

'I haven't been around such a desirable woman in months, Doc. What if I do grow anxious and lose control?'

'You have Bruno to watch over you. If you experience even the slightest inkling of a problem, make an excuse to leave the table and have Bruno take you back to your room — at least get you out of sight.'

'I hate being weak and vulnerable, Doc. I can't have anyone see me

69

. . . well, you know.'

'The recent findings of a London neurologist named Jackson suggested the medical condition might be brought on by brief electro-chemical discharges in the brain. But, as yet, there is no known treatment in the medical world as to how to subdue such impulses. We can only hope future experiments lead to a more reliable cure. Until then, all I can offer you is the potassium bromide.'

'I know, Doc, and it's the reason why I continue to have all of the most recent medical journals and articles sent here, to help keep you up to date. If any new procedures are found, I want to know about it the very minute you do.'

'I've no reason not to be totally honest with you, Mr Huntley,' Lyndell said. 'You offered me a haven when I was a fugitive. I owe you my freedom.'

Huntley smiled, reasonably satisfied he could handle the upcoming meeting without incident. 'You've certainly earned your keep, Doc. I've no complaints.'

'I have an order for pharmaceuticals

and other supplies,' Lyndell told him. 'Belva will bring it in with her tomorrow morning.'

'I'm sure I can get everything you want. Our supplier in Santa Fe has a solid inventory.'

'Then I'll say good night, Mr Huntley. I promised Belva I would take her out to dinner.'

'At the Refectory?'

'No, the Mexican tavern. Belva is quite fond of their 'Fiesta Special' meal.'

'Ah, refried beans, Spanish rice and enchiladas.'

Lyndell showed a rare smile. 'She likes to say she's adding spice to her personality.'

'She's quite a charming lady already,' Huntley observed. 'You're lucky to have someone who thinks enough of you to follow you here.'

'I feel guilty about that,' he replied. 'She had a good job at the bank and a number of friends — even a sister in Golden, Colorado. I'm to blame for her having come to this criminal oasis.'

Huntley displayed a rare compassion. 'I'd say she thinks you are worth the sacrifice, Doc.'

'She believes in my innocence.'

'As do I,' Huntley told him. 'However, my word or support would do little to clear your name. Operating this purgatory for outlaws and wealthy misfits is not exactly the prerequisite for a saint.'

Lyndell lifted a hand in farewell and left the room. Once he had gone, Huntley went to his closet and removed the freshly laundered and pressed suit jacket and pants. He wanted to make a good impression on the lady writer. With a degree of luck and charm, this social encounter might lead to a more personal conquest. The notion caused his heart rate to increase. He set his teeth . . .

Easy there, Jason old boy, he warned. *Take it slow and easy; you need to keep your head and emotions under control. It wouldn't do to make a scene tonight.*

4

Amy wrote some more of her story before getting ready for her dinner meeting with Huntley. In spite of being terrified earlier, she resolved to move forward. The pages were filling up effortlessly and she had yet to meet the mystery writer of the cryptic letter. When the appointed hour drew near, she set aside her writing materials and put on her nicest dress. For the next few minutes she fussed over making herself as presentable as possible. She was ready when she heard steps in the hallway. Before Whitney had a chance to knock, she quickly moved over and pulled open the door. He was caught with his knuckles raised and quickly lowered the hand to his side.

'Must be my big feet,' he said. 'Didn't know you were such a keen detective that you would know it was me from hearing my steps.'

Amy said, 'I assumed you would be punctual. It's five minutes before the hour.'

He took in her appearance at a glance and backed up a step to allow her into the hallway. 'If a gal like you was offering to have dinner with me, I'd wait for you until crows turn white and dogs learn to fly.'

She laughed at the comment and moved out next to Whitney. He reached past her and closed the door. She paused to take a deep breath and let it out slowly.

'I must admit, I'm a trifle nervous about this meeting.' She straightened and squared her shoulders, 'But let's not keep Mr Huntley waiting. This is what I wanted.'

Whitney offered her his arm to steady her going down the stairway. Wearing a bellowed-out skirt, she could not see her feet, let alone the stairs. She continued to hold on to his arm as they crossed the foyer and went out into the dusk.

'I'll stick around outside till you finish dinner,' Whitney told her, as they started to walk to the restaurant.

Amy shook her head. 'I'm sure Mr Huntley will be gentleman enough to see me back to my room.'

'If he does, I won't butt in. If he doesn't, I'll be on hand.'

'All right, Scotty,' she approved of his agenda. 'I'll feel more secure knowing you are nearby.'

He didn't speak again as they approached the entrance to the finely decorated eating place. Rather than leave her at the door, he escorted her inside. They stopped to look around the room, which was nearly filled with customers.

'Ah, Miss Cole,' a man dressed in an immaculate white suit advanced to meet them. 'I am James, maître d' of the Huntley Refectory. Mr Huntley arrived a few moments ago and has ordered a superior, yet fragile, red wine for this evening. May I see you to your table?'

Amy flicked a glance at Whitney. He gave her a nod of encouragement and stepped away, heading for the exit.

'Yes, thank you,' she told the man.

'We have several delicacies available for your dining pleasure tonight — roast mutton, braised venison or a petite pepper steak suitable for a lady's less robust appetite,' the man informed her professionally. As he spoke he led her past the rows of tables, to a sectioned-off corner of the dinning room, practically hidden from view.

Raised two steps higher than the main dining hall, the partitioned division had ceiling to floor curtains and a railing surrounding the enclosure. The drapery was open at the access to allow entrance for a guest or the attending waiter. She climbed the stairs and stopped on the small platform and stared at her host.

He was a well-dressed man, perhaps as old as thirty, but readily in his prime, with black, wavy hair, dark eyes and bushy brows. The man rose up from the elaborately decorated table — which was positioned beneath a crystal, candle-lit chandelier — standing for her approach. She found herself momentarily agape. Huntley was nothing like she had imagined. Far from a domineering despot with glaring, suspicious eyes and a sneer of cruelty pasted on his lips, the gentleman before her was strikingly handsome. He had a slightly pointed chin, an amiable, ready-to-smile mouth and a flawlessly waxed mustache set beneath a noble aquiline nose. He appeared physically fit and stood several inches taller than her petite five-foot-two frame.

'Miss Cole,' he said silkily, while his rich oak-colored eyes flashed over her with a perceptible approval. 'May I say it is a rare honor to have a celebrated author visit our fair town. And you are much more beautiful than I supposed from the mere glimpse I had of you when you arrived this morning by stagecoach.'

'Thank you for the kind words,' she

dismissed a portion of his flattery, 'but I'm hardly a renowned author.'

The maître d' held her chair and the two of them sat down. He then looked at Amy expectantly. 'If you would care to order now . . . ?'

'The roast mutton sounds good,' she told him. 'It's been ages since I've eaten meat other than beef or pork.'

'Very good,' he said. Either Huntley had already ordered or James knew what to bring him as he quickly left them alone.

'We weren't formally introduced, Miss Cole, but I am Jason Dante Huntley. Welcome to my tiny piece of the world.'

'It's very impressive, Mr Huntley,' she replied. 'I visited a fort once before and it was no larger than this place of yours. I'm amazed — it appears you have managed to encompass an entire town inside these walls.'

He took a moment to pour her a glass of rose-colored wine. When he spoke, he maintained a self-effacing air.

'It began as a simple trading post. As time passed and more travelers came this way, I was able to add a livery stable and build a hotel. The casino came next and I hired more people and expanded to include a general store. It was necessary to construct several bunkhouses for the hired help and I purchased animals for the stockyards. To fulfill the growing demand, I built two more boarding houses, a tavern, bakery and this restaurant. In the past year we've added a barber, a shoe and clothing shop . . . and finally, we were able to open a pharmacy, with a genuine doctor to serve our community.'

'And the twelve-foot wall with guards posted at the gates?'

'There were still Comanche and Apache raiding parties when I started out. The wall was extended each time we added another building. That's no easy task, considering the timber has to come from a mill located fifty miles away.'

'I would like to discuss this fortress of yours in more detail.'

'For one of your books?'

'Yes,' she answered. 'I don't intend to start writing true stories of the West, but it would be a plus for my books if I could state they were based on fact.'

'It's taken me seven years to build my Babylon in the desert. And while I rather fancy the idea of advertising, I wouldn't want the presence of some of our clientele to be made public. It might cause enough stir within the territorial government to invite them to act against us.'

'Because you harbor so many wanted criminals?'

He smiled, beguiling her with a savvy gaze. 'In essence, yes, but I imagine you have an exaggerated notion of the *criminals* we serve here.' He pointed to a couple across the room. 'Mr and Mrs George Hytower, he's the brother-in-law of a California congressman — he convinced other investors to put money into a venture that turned out to be a hoax. The lady you see waiting tables burned down the house of a woman who slept with her husband. No one was hurt, but the husband chose to side with the other woman. The old gent who runs your hotel — Henry — he protected a man who was being assaulted in his hotel in Kansas. Hit the assailant over the head to keep him from hurting the patron. The problem is, the man died from the head injury and happened to be related to a powerful banker. Even our town doctor had to pick up and leave his practice because someone accused him of murder. Many of the criminals here are victims of unfair circumstances or biased lawmen and judges.'

'Did you also have to run from the law? Is that why you set up out here in the middle of nowhere?'

He laughed. 'How rare to find someone so forthright and honest. You do realize I have the authority to prevent anyone from entering or leaving this place?'

She blinked at the warning although he continued to smile. 'The answer is no,' he went on to answer her question, 'I was not on the run from the law. However, I happened on to a situation where I ended up with a lot more money than I ever expected to have. To prevent anyone from taking it from me, I hired a couple good men and started a trading post. The growth of Babylon continued as the reputation of my fortress grew and the population increased.'

The meal was served and they stuck to idle conversation between bites. Jason was quite charming and kept her smiling from stories about people who came to his fortress. She could have listened to him for hours, wishing only that she had a pen and paper handy to copy down some of the many tales verbatim.

Dessert was ice cream over apple cobbler and she was truly amazed that they could offer such exceptional cuisine. When she mentioned it, Jason shrugged it off.

'We receive a shipment of ice via specially designed ice wagons every week. We also buy fruit from shippers as far away as California. If you want an apple or an orange, you can buy one at the general store — about a dollar each.'

'Gracious! I don't think I'll be buying any fruit right away.'

'Then enjoy the dessert — it's premium priced, but our frequent guests consist of numerous affluent men and women. That's why I decided to call this place Little Babylon . . . after a fabled city that rose from the dust to become the most powerful city in the world.' He displayed a humorous grin, 'Well, for a short time anyway.'

'I can't be certain, but isn't one translation of the word Babylon *garden of the gods* or something like that?'

Jason laughed out loud. 'You are a scholar, dear lady. I doubt more than a few people within a hundred miles know that detail.'

'I once had a character I was going to

call Babylon Bonnie . . . until I decided it was a bit too outlandish.'

'Perhaps, but it does sound colorful.'

'Back to the goods you have transported here, I can readily understand why everything is expensive. However, I'm a little surprised at the caliber of people, especially those who are not actually on the run from the law.'

'People come here from all over the country to do business because we afford them a degree of privacy as well as luxury. The people here know this is a safe haven, albeit an expensive place to stay.'

'I don't suppose there are any vagrants within these walls?'

'Anyone who causes trouble or doesn't pay his bill is escorted beyond the gate and told not to come back. If someone breaks the law, I preside over the hearing and pronounce sentence. It has to be that way, there has to be order and control.'

'I should think that would be a tall order, considering you allow bandits, rustlers, killers and thieves to seek shelter here.'

'They pay for the privilege and know to be on their best behavior.'

'And what about you? How is it you don't have a stunning and refined woman at your side?'

'The thought has been on my mind lately. I don't suppose you know a beautiful, intelligent, charming young lady who might be interested?' He watched her carefully, as if to measure her response. 'I would make such a woman my queen and she would want for nothing.'

'You are surrounded by a barren wilderness.' Amy kept a lightness in her tone. 'To be housed in a palace would make this existence no less a prison.'

'You call it a prison, but many of the people who live here are workers I've hired. The chef once worked in San Francisco, my sentries are ex-soldiers or lawmen. I pay the highest wages for many services we have here.

'As for being trapped or confined, it

is but a day's ride to the railroad. From there, the entire world is open to a person's wishes or desires. Some of my employees make more in a few months than they could elsewhere in several years.'

'So you do travel?'

'On occasion,' he responded, 'although I am quite satisfied here. This is my home.'

'With so much to offer, it is even more surprising you don't have a lady companion.'

Jason appeared ready to reply to her comment, but stopped short. He began to rub either side of his head with his hands. She was about to ask if he was getting a headache, but his expression turned apprehensive and a degree of alarm entered his eyes. He quickly looked about the room, then stood up.

'Mr Huntley?' Amy said. 'Are you all right? Is something wrong?'

Suddenly a large man appeared. He wore regular work clothes, with no hat to cover his completely bald head. He quickly pulled the curtain closed and hurried around to open a concealed door behind the table.

'Excuse me,' Jason barely uttered the words, 'I must go.'

The man put his arm around Jason and guided him out the door. 'Mr Huntley will talk to you tomorrow,' the large man grunted over his shoulder, as if speaking was something that did not come naturally to him.

Amy sat dumbfounded at the table, her mouth agape, wondering what had just happened. Before she had time to get her thought process working the curtain parted again and the maître d' appeared, looking at her impassively.

'Is there anything else you would like this evening, Miss Cole?' he asked, as if nothing was amiss.

'Has something happened? Is Mr Huntley all right?' she asked.

'Of course,' he replied. 'I believe he was needed for some kind of emergency. Bruno interrupts his meals or conversations from time to time. It's not my place to question his actions, but I'm sure Mr Huntley will explain it to you the next time you get together.'

She wasn't convinced by his story, but being a guest, she kept further questions to herself. 'I'm finished,' she said. 'It was a fabulous meal, the best I've had since I left Saint Louis.'

'I shall pass along your compliment to the chef. He works very hard to prepare each and every meal.'

'It was very impressive.'

'If you would like, you may use the exit behind you. It leads to the alleyway between the restaurant and the casino.'

'Thank you, but my escort will be watching for me at the front door.'

The head waiter bade her farewell and she made her way out to the street. Whitney was there to greet her on the walk. He cast an inquisitive gaze past her as she approached.

'Did you say something to make Huntley angry with you?'

'It was very bizarre, Scotty,' she replied, stepping over to his side. 'I didn't see anyone signal him, but he suddenly got up and left at the end of the meal. He did apologize, but it was very strange.'

'Nothing happening out here on the streets that I could see,' Whitney said. 'Must have been something private.'

'I can only assume his personal guard gestured to him. He arrived from out of nowhere, put an arm around Huntley, and the two of them left by a back door.'

'This personal guard, he a flashy dresser with a fancy pistol on either hip?'

'Not even close. This guy had no more hair than a hen's egg, was half-again as large as you and kind of grunted his words.'

Whitney ended his questions and said, 'Don't have any idea what it means, but it's one strange man who invites a beautiful woman to dinner and then abandons her.'

They continued back to the hotel. Upon reaching Amy's room, Whitney pushed open the door and took a quick look inside the room. She thought it an unnecessary precaution, but it did add to her feeling of security.

'What's the plan for tomorrow?' he asked. 'I need to do some looking around town and see if the Polson boys are here.'

'I didn't get a chance to ask about them,' Amy told him apologetically. 'With the meal ending so abruptly I hardly got to question him at all.'

'That's all right. You've got your original case to worry about. I don't want you saying something to raise the man's suspicions about me.'

'I intend to speak to the doctor tomorrow and see what I can find out.'

'I saw him and a woman walking arm-in-arm toward a café or tavern down the street. At least I heard someone call him doctor when they walked by.'

'The woman is probably the person who wrote the letter. I imagine she will try to contact me once she knows I'm in town.'

'Sounds like you're ready to begin your detective work.'

Amy found herself staring into those mystical, cloudy-colored eyes. 'I'm glad you're here,' she murmured. 'I wouldn't want to be doing this alone.'

Whitney displayed an easy grin. 'Maybe you'll put me in your next book,' he teased. 'I could be the lovesick gent you leave behind at the end.'

'You think my character, Tess, would do that?'

'How else can she continue wooing men in future stories?' he made his point. 'I don't recall ever seeing any titles where it included 'Mrs Jones' or 'the wife of so-and-so' — the gals are all single and independent.'

'You're right, of course. The heroine must have a new romance in each book to satisfy the readers.'

'Do you want me to be around for breakfast?' He changed the subject and backed out of the room.

'No, I ate enough tonight to last me till at least noon tomorrow. You are free to do whatever you like while I seek out the doctor and the mystery writer. Just promise you'll be careful.'

'I'll be around when you need me,' Whitney said and gave a slight tip of his head as a goodnight.

After the door closed, she knew he waited in the hallway until she pushed home the bolt on the lock. Once again she thanked providence for having such a man come into her life.

Still recovering from the long stage ride and lack of rest, Amy fell asleep almost as soon as her head hit the pillow. But what seemed moments later, a violent crashing sound awakened her with a start. Before she could sit up there came a piercing *bang! bang! bang!* — the sound of gunfire! Three shots in quick succession sounded from the hallway!

Amy threw off her blankets and jumped to her feet. She scrambled across the room and put her ear to the door. There were shouts from downstairs and out on the street, along with the retreating steps of someone going down the hall and taking the back stairs.

Her heart pounded so hard it caused her to shake with each beat. *Whitney!* was her first concern. She pulled back the bolt and eased open the door.

Henry appeared at the top of the stairs, panting from his haste, a shotgun gripped in his hands. He had obviously been in bed as he wore his night shirt over trousers. Two other men came up behind him, both of them carrying pistols.

'Which room?' the one man asked.

Henry pointed down the hall. 'Looks like the second one past the lady's . . . ' He paused to flash a quick look at Amy before he finished, 'that would be Scotty's room.'

The news hit Amy like a doubled fist in the solar plexus. She quickly threw on her robe and entered the hall, following along behind the three men. The door to Whitney's room had been kicked or bashed open by force. Henry stuck his head inside and pulled back at once.

'Damn! They blasted him plum full of holes,' he stated sadly. 'Can't hardly see the body for all the blood.'

A second man confirmed his evaluation. 'Poor bugger didn't know what hit him.'

'Never give him a chance,' Henry agreed.

A thick blackness swirled before Amy's eyes, threatening to engulf her senses. She braced a hand against the wall to keep from fainting. Whitney — he'd been killed!

5

A gent poked his head out from across the hall. 'I heard the shooter,' he announced. 'Busted down the door and fired three times. Then he made like a jack-rabbit and scooted down the back stairs. He was gone before I could get a look at him.'

Henry noticed Amy had come out in the hallway and quickly turned to her. 'You best not be seeing this, missy,' he said gently. 'One of the bullets hit your friend in the face. It's not a pretty sight.'

'The fellow is deader than boot leather,' one of the men, who had entered the room, declared softly. 'Hit him once in the head and two to the chest. I reckon the gent didn't know what hit him.'

Just then another man came up to the top of the stairs. He stopped, seeing the crowded corridor. 'What's going on?' he asked. 'Were those gunshots I heard from down on the street?'

Amy knew that voice! She whirled about, took three steps to reach the new arrival and threw her arms around his neck. 'Whit — ' Although choked with emotion, she remembered to change the name. 'Scotty!' She gasped, unable to stop the flood of tears. 'We thought it was you!'

'What the hell?' Henry had trailed after Amy. 'There's a man who's done been kilt in your room, Scotty. Want to tell me how come it ain't you?'

Whitney had to talk around Amy's full head of hair, as her grip was akin to a kitten clinging to the only pole sticking up in a millpond.

'After those two morons tried to force their way into the lady's room this afternoon, I wanted to be closer at hand. I asked Fancy Dan to trade rooms with me. I was going to tell you about it earlier, but you were not at the counter.'

'He's right,' one of the men spoke up,

surveying inside his old room. 'I recognize Fancy Dan's gambling suit draped over the dressing table. He left the game early because he wasn't feeling good.'

'Turned out to be a fatal ailment,' the other man spoke up.

'If I find out who did this, I'll sure enough give him a horizontal ride to the graveyard,' Henry vowed. 'No one gets away with coming into my place to harm one of my guests!'

Amy gathered her composure, released her hold on Whitney and stepped back. 'I'm sorry,' she murmured. 'I didn't mean to react so . . . so . . .'

'Passionately?' Whitney finished wryly.

His teasing helped her to recover her poise. '*Emotionally* is the word I was going to use,' she recovered. 'It's hard to find a decent help. I would have hated to lose a couple days from my writing just to replace you.'

'Be a real inconvenience for me as well,' he jibed back.

'Thing is,' Henry piped up, 'who was

this bushwhacking jasper after — you or Fancy Dan?'

'Does the gambler have any enemies?' Whitney asked.

'Not to my knowledge. But any time a man wins more than he loses at games of chance he makes enemies.'

'I just arrived in town, so I can't imagine anyone being mad enough to want to kill me.'

'Except for Skeet and Ike,' Henry suggested.

'I don't think so,' Whitney replied. 'We parted on pretty good terms.'

He bobbed his head. 'Yeah, you did talk your way around a fight. Been me you knocked down the stairs, I'd have been for giving you a thorough whupping.'

'I'll remember to walk careful around you if we meet on the steps,' Whitney told him.

A new figure appeared at the head of the stairs. Whitney recognized Nickel at once. The man marched past them and went into the dead man's room. He returned a few seconds later and confronted Whitney.

'We ain't had a killing in two months, honcho,' he stated the fact. 'You arrive on the stage and a man is shot in his sleep the very same night!'

'I had nothing to do with it.'

'That's true enough, Nickel,' one of the men vouched for Whitney. 'I passed him on the street right before we heard the shots and I came upstairs with Jake.'

'You heard the shooting?'

'I'm staying down on the ground floor and we were right outside the hotel,' he explained. 'Only problem is, we came in the front whilst the shooter was going out the back way. No one got a look at him.'

'Why would anyone kill Fancy Dan?'

'Scotty and Dan traded rooms earlier, so Dan might not have been the intended victim,' Henry said, filling Nickel in about the switch.

'Who do you know in town?' Nickel questioned Whitney. 'Who would want you dead?'

'To my knowledge, the stage driver is the only man I know in Little Babylon,' Whitney answered truthfully. 'He's a friend. Other than him, I've never met any of the people in town.'

'Anyone hear of Fancy having any beef or trouble with anyone?' Nickel asked the group.

'He was a slick card player, but I always figured him to be a square-shooter,' one of the men replied.

'Same here, I never heard anyone call him a cheat,' the other agreed.

Nickel looked over at Amy. 'What about you, lady?' he queried. 'This killing happened on your first night in town too. Are you here for some special reason?'

'I wanted to see this place and meet Mr Huntley.'

He didn't look convinced. 'You made a long train and stage ride to take a gander at an outlaw fortress.'

'It's for her books,' Whitney took up for her. 'She wants to put some realism in her writing.'

'*Realism?*' Nickel grinned. 'Guess I'm not the only one who can use highfalutin' words.'

'My mother was a school teacher until she married my father and moved to a ranch. Whilst there was only my brother and me around, she never did quit teaching.'

Nickel eyed him with a skeptical look. 'You're more than you pretend to be, Scotty,' and, diverting his gaze to Amy, 'and so are you, lady. I don't know what you two are up to yet, but I'll find out the truth.'

'I'd rather you find out who killed the gambler,' Whitney said, 'in case it was someone gunning for me.'

Nickel directed his attention toward the men standing next to Henry. 'You two wrap Fancy in a blanket and haul his carcass over to the carpenter's place. I'll round up Cyrus and we'll talk to anyone who might have seen our killer exit down the back way. Being as the rear door is mostly used when a man is going to the livery, I don't hold out a lot of hope we'll find a witness.'

Amy took Whitney's hand. 'Would you come into my room for a moment, Scotty. I need to go over our schedule for tomorrow.'

'Yes, ma'am,' he answered, stepping over to hold the door for her.

Once Amy was inside, he entered and closed the door. She could not hide her apprehension, speaking to him in a hushed and excited tone of voice.

'Do you think someone intended to kill you, Scotty? Could those killers know you are here?'

'I don't see how. When I was on the ranch, we had heard of the Polson gang, but I've never seen any of them.'

Amy paced the floor. 'I didn't expect this,' she admitted. 'Fighting and killing — it's more than I bargained for.'

'You did come to a bandit stronghold, ma'am,' Whitey reminded her.

'Yes, but — '

'We don't know anything for certain,' he interrupted her. 'Perhaps someone wanted to be rid of Fancy Dan. If he mentioned he had traded rooms, it would give them an opening to kill him and have Nickel suspect I was the actual target.'

Amy was not convinced. 'I don't know. Those men made it sound as if Fancy Dan had no enemies.'

'An enemy doesn't always declare himself out in the open, especially when he intends to kill someone.'

She looked him in the eye. 'Why weren't you in your room?'

'I went to one of the saloons to see if I could pick up anything on the Polson boys.'

'And did you?'

'No. I bought a drink and sat around keeping watch, but I didn't hear anything worthwhile or see a trio who might be the brothers I'm looking for.'

'And you're sure none of them would recognize you?'

'Don't see how they could. Like I said, I've never met any of them.'

Amy still suffered a nervous stomach from the shooting. Her fear that

Whitney had been killed had turned her inside out. She tried to shake the feeling, but the concern was real. What if someone had tried to kill him? What if she ended up responsible for his death?

'I-I wonder if this wasn't a mistake — for both of us.'

Whitney arched his brows. 'You sorry for hiring me?'

'No, I mean the coming here, the searching for answers and killers. I never thought — I mean the two ruffians tried to enter my room and now a man is killed — it puts the mere writing of a story in perspective.'

'Tornado Tess would laugh in the face of danger,' he reminded her.

Amy swallowed her uncertainty and flashed a smile. 'Yes, silly me, allowing reason and sanity to enter my thinking.'

He winked at her. 'Sure can't permit something like that, not with a fearless female detective looking to save the day.'

'I guess not.'

'Don't be concerned about me,' he said. 'Remember, I was on my way here before I met you. You're not responsible for my welfare. If I get myself killed, it's because I came here looking for justice.'

'And I also have a case to solve,' she recouped her bravado.

Whitney searched her face. 'It might be out of line to say so, but I was right surprised by your reaction to my not being dead. A man might read something into the . . . *emotional*' — he used her own word — 'display you exhibited, when you learned I was not the man killed tonight.'

'I was naturally relieved,' Amy offered a rebuttal. 'True or not, I would have felt responsible for your death.'

'That's all it was?'

'What else could it have been?'

Whitney shrugged. 'I was kind of hoping you were developing a hankering for me.'

'Hankering?' Amy put on a teasing mien. 'You mean like the desire to buy ice cream at a town festival?'

'I was thinking more the way your Tornado Tess began to think about Trapper Joe in your book.'

'Trapper Joe saved her life — after she had saved his. They were mutually beholden to one another.'

'Mutually beholden,' he repeated the words. 'Is that what it takes before a man is worthy to hold your hand?'

'Is that your new goal in life, Scotty? You want to hold my hand?'

'Among other things,' he admitted.

'Wasn't it you who said we needed to maintain a degree of professionalism?'

'That was before I knew you had feelings for me.'

'I explained how I felt,' she argued. 'I would have thought myself responsible for your death. It's not something I would like on my conscience.'

'And that's all?'

'Of course that's all,' she said with some conviction. 'I hardly know you.'

'We did spend the night together,' he reminded her.

'I don't think sharing the same

uncomfortable coach during an over-night ride counts for much.'

Whitney continued to study her, as if searching for the faintest sign of what — Weakness? Affection? Amy held herself rigid and refused to let emotion enter her expression. After a long few seconds, he took a step back to the door.

'It wouldn't do to start any gossip about my being in your room,' he said. 'I'll say good night.'

Amy couldn't summon words, fearful she would stop him from leaving. When he was gone and the door closed, she sighed and shoved the lock in place. For a brief span of time she stood there, wondering if she had handled the encounter correctly.

She could not deny the immediate dread she experienced when she thought Whitney had been killed, nor the elation at discovering he was still alive. Such dramatic mood swings, yet she was uncertain as to how she really felt about the man. Standing firm, she had faced the challenge in his scrutiny. Had she shown even a minute degree of interest or frailty, what would have happened?

She was struck numb as a vivid conclusion leapt to mind. *I would have ended up in his arms, crushed against his chest and been kissed into blissful submission!*

Amy recoiled from a warm flush which engulfed her senses. She immediately cursed the girlish notions over the uncontrollable physical reaction. What a lot of romantic nonsense! She was not looking for a man; she was searching for a story and trying to unravel a mystery at the same time. There was no time for fawning over a mildly attractive, somewhat stimulating cowboy. Whitney had caught her at a weak moment, that's all it was.

'He was right about one thing,' she murmured to herself, 'Tornado Tess would know how to handle this kind of situation.' With a harsher tone, 'As for you, Amanda Jane Cole, your feelings and imagination have run wild!'

6

Whitney was up early and on his own. After a quick bite, he strolled the length of Little Babylon and back. Obviously a more lively place at night, there were few people on the streets before the sun reached a mid-morning level.

After picking up his laundry and returning it to his room, Whitney spent a couple hours moving from place to place and simply watching. The storekeepers opened their doors, the barber was doing a good business and the fortress took on the appearance of a normal town. There were a few people coming and going through the main gate — some were stopped and questioned while others were waved on. Probably the regulars didn't have to explain their visits or departures, while the new guests were told the rules or more closely scrutinized.

Nickel appeared on the walk and wandered over to stand at his side. Neither spoke for a time, both watching the activity at the main gate.

'You wondering if the man who tried to kill you last night is leaving town?' Nickel finally broke the silence.

'I don't know that anyone tried to kill me,' Whitney replied.

'You came here for a reason, Scotty — or whatever your real name is. I'm responsible for keeping the peace here and I take my job seriously.'

Whitney rotated about to meet the man's inquisitive look. Not a man he wanted for an enemy, yet he didn't know how far to trust him as an ally.

'I've been wondering how things worked here, Nickel. You obviously stop newcomers at the gate. How do you determine who stays and who goes?'

'First off, we inform them of how much it costs to stay here. You've likely noticed the high price tag on most things and services. You don't come in unless you've got the money to pay.

Most are willing to spend a great deal for the security and protection we offer.'

'Yeah, two bucks for a hair cut? I didn't bother to give the barber a tip.'

'Huntley acts as a banker of sorts. For security, most every man or woman who comes here with a lot of money leaves a portion or all of it with the boss. To discourage robbery or theft, Huntley provides a customer with scrip, like they use in mining towns, and they spend it until it's gone. Some prefer to use their own money, and that's fine too.'

'I can see where the use of scrip would eliminate a lot of temptation for robbers.'

Nickel bobbed his head, 'Plus people need only draw what they intend to spend. The casino keeps a running total so you can pick up scrip against your account any time day or night.'

'Very smart operation.'

'And Huntley intends that we keep Babylon as peaceful as possible. He has big plans for turning this town into a haven for the rich — criminal or not.' He grinned, 'Hence the reason he pays me so well.'

'Supposing a man had a score to settle and it happened to be with someone staying within the walls of Little Babylon? What are your rules about something like that?'

'Lawmen and bounty hunters are not allowed inside the fortress.'

'How about a personal vendetta?'

'We've worked through a few disagreements in the past,' the man answered. 'As long as it's a fair fight and no one else gets hurt, we let the hand play out without interference.'

'And if one of the people was important or had a lot of money to spend? Would that make a difference?'

Nickel regarded Whitney more closely. 'This personal vendetta, it wouldn't be concerning Huntley himself?'

'No, I've never met him.'

'Then you ought to clear your intended action with me first. So long as you're not a US Marshal or a killer for hire, I'll see to it you get your chance.'

'You'd do that, just put us in a room together and let us go at it?'

'Something like that.'

'And if the man with the most money died, Huntley would be a little bit richer.'

Nickel smiled. 'Now you understand why we don't prevent retribution in special cases. Why don't you tell me who you're looking for and why?'

'I don't know,' Whitney resisted the idea. 'What if the guy went to you or Huntley and offered a sizable amount to take his side? How do I know you wouldn't help him get the job done?'

The man dismissed the idea. 'I work for Huntley and handle his security, but the man wouldn't risk his reputation by condoning a murder or ambush within the walls of Babylon.'

'I'm not sure the guy I'm looking for is in Babylon.'

'Someone tried to kill you last night,

Scotty. Seems to me the fella might already know you are in town.'

'You can't be certain they weren't after Fancy Dan.'

'I'm looking into it, but Fancy has been our guest off and on for the better part of two years. He's never even been involved in an argument. The man was a professional gambler, but he was also a well-respected gentleman. I don't buy the idea he was the target. No, you're the man the killer was looking for.'

Whitney didn't argue. 'If you're right, it would mean someone already knows I'm here. It's a good bet I might need some help to have any chance at a fair fight.'

'You think on it and let me know what you want to do, Scotty,' he said. 'Just don't start anything without telling me first. You best sidestep trouble until I give the go ahead.'

'I will if I have the chance.'

A man walked over from the gate to where they were standing. He had stringy blond hair hanging from beneath a sombrero-style straw hat, wore a gun tied low and walked with a swagger. On his vest was a metal badge with the word 'Regulator' on it.'

'Jess Haversack is at the gate,' he informed Nickel. 'Claims he has a wad of money this trip.'

'Man doesn't learn,' Nickel replied. 'What's he going to do about being kicked out last month for betting money he didn't have?'

'He says he'll make the debt good.'

'You know what this means, Cyrus. Someone is on his back trail.'

'I expect you're right.'

'All right, let him in, but make damn sure he pays what he owes and stays within his limits. He ends up in the hole to us a second time and we'll turn him over to the law or whoever is after him.'

Cyrus gave a bob of his head and returned to the gate.

'How many regulators are there in town?' Whitney asked Nickel.

'Just me and Cyrus, along with Bruno when he's needed,' the man answered. 'If it comes to trouble, I can call on Skeet and Ike. They can't think on their own but they do as they are told.'

'Only five men altogether. What if someone like the Dalton Gang showed up with fifteen men?'

'The guards from around town are all available too. We have sixteen men working rotating shifts — there's always three or four at the main gate and another couple roving the streets. The Dalton Gang wouldn't stand a chance against our twenty armed men.'

'Like I said, I'll sure try to let you know if I intend any action within the walls of Babylon.'

Nickel laughed and moved on down the walk.

★   ★   ★

It took some maneuvering, but Amy was able to catch Belva as she left Huntley's office and walked toward the nearest eatery. She fell in alongside the woman before she reached the door of the small canteen.

'Can I join you for breakfast?' she asked. 'I so hate eating alone.'

A glimmer of recognition entered Belva's eyes. 'Tess?' she queried in a hushed voice.

'Amanda Cole,' Amy replied. 'Tess is a character in my books — the ones you've been reading.'

'You' — she did not hide her surprise — 'you know who I am?'

'You're the lady who wrote for my help.'

Belva was obviously impressed by her deduction. 'Yes, I'd very much like to have breakfast at the same table.'

Before the basic Breakfast Special was finished, the two of them had discussed a number of subjects. It turned serious as they sipped the tea they had ordered with the meal.

'You claim the doctor was framed,' Amy stated. 'Tell me exactly what happened.'

Belva appeared to sort out her

thoughts and put the details in order before she began. Even then, she glanced around to make sure no one else was within hearing distance.

'Doctor Lyndell had a good practice in Colorado Springs. We became friends and it grew into more than friendship. He's a widower with only a daughter who moved back east with her husband some years back. I — well, the first man I loved died in the War Between the States, and so I've never been married.

'Anyway, Ralph treated a woman for cracked ribs and some facial injuries — not the first time for this particular woman, as her husband had a temper and drank too much too often. One night, a couple weeks after the injuries occurred, he was summoned to visit her house.

'Ralph arrived to find the woman's husband both drunk and remorseful, while the lady had been knocked unconscious. He had barely begun to administer treatment to the woman when her husband was shot from outside an open window. The gun was tossed into the room and the shooter ran away.'

'What did Doctor Lyndell do?'

'He tried to save the life of the husband, but the man was mortally wounded and died. Before Ralph had time to contact the authorities, a city policeman arrived and arrested him for murder.'

'Didn't he tell him about the shooter?'

'The gun was on the floor and a passer-by said he had heard the shot but didn't see anyone outside of the house.'

'How did Lyndell escape?'

'I used my savings and posted his bail — a judge allowed it so Ralph could continue to tend to his patients. We left town the day before the hearing concerning a trial.'

'What prompted you to come here?'

'A news story was printed in the Colorado Springs newspaper about the bandit stronghold where no law dared enter. Ralph was one of several doctors in nearby towns who received an invitation to visit. It seems Mr Huntley was searching for a physician to come work for him.'

Amy filed the coincidence away and continued with her investigation. 'You said Doctor Lyndell was called to the house to treat the injured lady.' At her nod, a second question, 'The husband was drunk and apologetic. Had he sent for the doctor?'

'He said a young boy, something of a town runner, came to fetch him,' Belva replied. 'I don't know who sent him. Does it matter?'

'We need to find out if he was on a paid errand, if the husband sent him, or if he just happened to hear the fighting. It might be important.'

'I'll ask Ralph and see if he knows.'

'What about your situation here? How did you end up running the pharmacy?'

'We came to Little Babylon because

Ralph assumed he could continue to practice medicine. We only had a little money between us, but we knew there was no law and the town had been trying to recruit a doctor. Mr Huntley met with us and offered us the job of running the town pharmacy. Ralph also renders his services as a doctor, while I keep the accounting records for Mr Huntley.'

'It sounds like a good arrangement for both sides.'

'Yes, although I believe Mr Huntley may have had an ulterior motive for being so generous.'

'Oh? And what is that?'

Belva frowned. 'I can't be certain, because Ralph does not discuss his patients' problems with me. He's a very honorable man that way.'

'Tell me what you suspect.'

'Every week Ralph takes his medical bag and goes to Huntley's office. He stays for about an hour and then returns. He has never told me what goes on, but I have noticed he takes a bottle of potassium bromide from our stock with him each time. We routinely have a supply of the drug come in each month.'

'Do you know what the medication is for?'

'I once asked Ralph about it and he said it was used as a sedative. I suppose Mr Huntley might have trouble sleeping or some such thing.'

Amy had no knowledge of the drug or its uses but she decided she would try to find out more from Huntley. However, it would explain why he was sending invitations to nearby cities in an effort to enlist a doctor. As for his personal situation — if he had a medical condition — it was doubtful it was tied to anything that would help clear Doctor Lyndell's name.

'You said a passer-by heard the shot that killed the abusive husband?'

'Yes.'

'Do you know his or her name?'

'No, only that they told the story to the policeman who arrived.'

'And the same policeman arrested the doctor for murder,' Amy stated. 'What was the name of the policeman?'

'Officer Lowe — Victor Lowe. He's been with the Colorado Springs police for a couple years. Ralph believes he is an honorable man.'

Amy pulled a piece of paper and pencil from her pocket and made a note of the name. 'I need for you to find out whatever you can about the boy who came to fetch the doctor for the injured woman. It might be important. I'll have to find a way to get information about the witness and Policeman Lowe.'

'I'll ask Ralph about it and get back to you. However, I don't see how the boy or witness can help.'

'You don't believe the doctor would actually shoot anyone, do you?' Amy asked, ignoring her statement.

'Never. He's about the most mild-mannered person I ever met.'

'And did the policeman search around outside the windows for any sign of the actual shooter?'

'I don't know.'

'And you never learned of any other witnesses?'

'Only the one who spoke to the policeman.'

'I can't imagine anyone pointing a finger at the doctor — especially when he was trying to save the shooting victim's life. Who would shoot someone and then try to save them?'

'It was clear they were going to prosecute Ralph. We left before the hearing, but he was the only one they arrested. I'm certain they would have found him guilty.'

'Running makes him look guilty too,' Amy pointed out. 'We will have to deal with that issue.'

'How?'

'By finding whoever it was who did the shooting and putting them behind bars.'

'But you're not really Tornado Tess, you're a writer!' Belva exclaimed. 'I wrote to you hoping you might give me some idea as to how to prove Ralph's innocence. I thought you might know a good attorney or judge. I never expected you to go searching for some mad killer on your own.'

Amy allowed a simper to play along her lips. 'Oh, you needn't worry about me. I'm not thinking of tackling a chore like this all by myself.'

7

The livery stable turned out to be where Whitney got the information he needed. By entering town with only a saddle, it made sense he would be needing a horse. That is, unless he took the stage when he left town. The man who ran the stable was showing him around when he spied several head of horses he recognized.

'That looks like a fair steed in the corner over there, the black with three white stockings and a striped forelock.'

'Yup, just picked up that little beauty. Some fellers showed up here with a herd of maybe fifty animals. They wouldn't sell me less than a dozen — probably ten more than I'll ever need, but they had a lot of fine horseflesh to sell. Got it cheap too, so I can make you a right good deal. What do you say to sixty dollars?'

'I think I saw the herd a few days back up north a way — the Polson brothers?'

'Can't say,' he replied. 'I only heard the names Jack and Tom.'

Whitney suffered an immediate setback. They had been here and left. He had missed them. Hiding his disappointment he asked, 'What happened to the rest of the herd?'

'Them boys headed the rest of the horses on down the trail. I reckon they intend to sell them to cattle ranches all the way to Santa Fe. How-some-whatsoever, they did say they would be back in a couple weeks to spend some of the money they were earning from the sales.'

'So they have been gone what, a few days?'

'Yup,' he said, frowning. 'Are you interested in a horse or not? You might get a better deal buying from those boys, but I doubt they are in the market to sell one horse at a time.'

'Tell you what,' Whitney said. 'I'll

give you five dollars to hold that black gelding for me. If I don't buy him when I leave, you keep the five. If I take him, put the five toward the price.'

'You've got some keen eyesight there, friend,' the stable owner said, squinting at him. 'I'll bet there ain't but a few men in the country can tell a gelding by looking at a horse from this distance.'

'I know a little about horses,' Whitney explained, 'and you sure wouldn't put a stallion in with a half-dozen mares.'

The man laughed. 'You got me there, son. I'll hold him for you till the end of the month. If you don't buy him by then I'll keep the five and sell him to the next buyer.'

'Fair enough.' Whitney handed him the money and headed back up the street.

★　★　★

Amy stopped on the walk as J.D. Huntley crossed the street. He wore an immaculate suit, string tie and a

128

businessman's hat. A wide smile of greeting spread across his face.

'Miss Cole,' he began, joining her on the wooden walkway, 'I'm so glad I was able to find you without having to send out a search party.'

She reciprocated with a simper of her own. 'Owning the town, I imagine you are kept informed of where every person is at any given time.'

'I wanted to apologize for the hasty departure last night,' he said, disregarding her comment. 'Something extremely urgent came up that I had to attend to immediately. I can't tell you how badly I feel for abandoning you at the table.'

'I was understandably concerned,' she admitted. 'I feared I might have said something offensive or — '

'No, no,' he assured her quickly. 'It had nothing to do with you. It's just that overseeing an entire town has demands and responsibilities. I am often called upon at a moment's notice.' He appeared to have memorized the line, as it was spoken perfectly, the way an actor might deliver a familiar line in a play.

'I'm glad I wasn't the cause of your leaving.'

'Can I make it up to you?' he asked. 'How about a tour of the town and then we can have lunch at one of our eating establishments?' Before she could give him an answer, he showed a winning smile again. 'We have some of the latest fashions at our new clothing store. It carries a variety of gowns, women's hats and jewelry . . . about anything a lady of quality would need.'

'That's extremely rare for a town located in the middle of a vast emptiness.'

'We do cater to a number of wealthy travelers,' he replied. 'And those men who bring a lady along like to treat them special.'

'I'd appreciate an escorted tour, but I need to let Scotty know where I am,' she said.

Huntley pointed down the street. 'By all means — I see he is coming this way.'

'Have you met my personal guardian?'

'No, but I do have everyone who comes here . . . scrutinized.'

'Scrutinized sounds better than investigated,' she said. 'Did you also scrutinize me?'

'Last night — personally.' He again displayed his winning smile. 'You are a person of supreme interest to me, one I should like to get to know much better.'

'Before you get too interested, I should tell you I have no intention of living out my life in a bandit stronghold.'

'This is an oasis, dear Amanda,' he corrected her. 'In time, I will add a grand hotel and build a theater that will draw performers from around the world. We'll offer magnificent casinos and restaurants of the highest caliber. There will be a weekly rodeo, carnivals and the finest clothes and dry goods available anywhere. Royalty and presidents will travel here to escape the ordinary life and enjoy seclusion from their responsibilities. We'll set up a shooting palace, with all manner of targets and weapons, carriage rides to picnic sites or fishing — there's a stream a couple miles from here. I promise you, this will one day become a haven for people to relax and be pampered.'

'It sounds as if it would take a lot of money to make your dream come true.'

'What you see here is only a start. As soon as the last of the hostile Indians are confined to reservations, the travelers will come. We'll run a spur to the railroad line and offer up special luxury cars for those visiting here.'

Whitney arrived but did not interrupt, waiting patiently for Amy to acknowledge his presence. She did so now.

'What do you think of such a colossal undertaking, Scotty?' she asked. 'Mr Huntley intends to make this a getaway for the affluent and powerful.'

'You only have two water towers,' Whitney pointed out. 'I would think you'll need access to more water, either by wells or pumps. There's also the fuel for heat and cooking stoves, lumber for building — the draftsmen and engineers, highly specialized craftsmen . . . ' He shook his head. 'It sounds like it would take a mountain of money to realize your dreams, Mr Huntley.'

The man took the rebuttal in his stride. 'When one embarks on a long journey, he need only begin with the first step. Each step after that draws him closer to his goal.'

'Well, I'd say you've definitely made the first step or two,' Whitney allowed. 'This stronghold appears to have most everything a person could ask for. It's an impressive place.'

Amy immediately thanked Whitney with an approving glance. While he was a horse rancher and a little rough around the edges, Whitney had a knack for interacting with other men. He had knocked down the two ruffians who came to her door and yet they had left without animosity. And now, speaking to the king of Little Babylon, he had expressed doubts about his plan, only to end the conversation with praise for his accomplishments.

'Mr Huntley is going to show me around and then we'll have something to eat,' Amy spoke to Whitney. 'Let's get together this afternoon and go over our schedule.'

'Whatever you say, Miss Cole.'

Huntley offered his arm and Amy took it. Whitney played his role and left them alone on the walk. She desperately wanted to talk to him about the case, but it would have to wait.

* * *

Nickel cornered Whitney while he was having something to eat. The man ordered the Wrangler Special and sat down next to him.

'Looks as if my boss is working extra hard to spark your boss,' he opened the conversation. 'Wonder if we won't both wind up working for the same side pretty quick.'

'I don't think Miss Cole intends to

live out here in the middle of nowhere.'

'Progress will soon have us more in contact with the rest of the world,' Nickel replied to that. 'We already have a telegraph and the surveyors have charted the route for a railroad spur. Huntley has friends in high places and enough money to make a lot of improvements.'

'Pretty high expectations for a bandit stronghold,' Whitney observed. 'Robbers and thieves must be doing a good business hereabouts.'

Nickel's meal arrived and he began to eat. 'Huntley is trying to make this more of a retreat or getaway for wealthy folks than a hideout for desperadoes. He has big plans.'

'If I were him I wouldn't add Miss Cole into those plans,' Whitney said. 'She has a passion for writing and I don't see her wanting to settle down in this fortress for the rest of her days.'

'Enough about our bosses, Scotty.' The man turned serious. 'I've checked out every man in town who played cards with Fancy Dan over the past few days. Nary a one had a grudge against him. Dan was a good player, but he didn't make a living at cards. His pa left him a bundle of money from a business back East. Every time he arrived in town, he would give us a bank note from a bank in Denver. The man played for the love of the game, not to win money. From what I've learned, everyone liked him — hell, who wouldn't like a guy with a lot of money who doesn't mind losing?'

'So whoever killed him was after me.'

'That's the way I read the cards — if you'll pardon the pun.' He grinned without humor. 'Also, we both know you aren't a simple bodyguard for the lady writer. You were already headed this way for a reason.'

Whitney studied the town regulator. Son of a preacher, his name on a Wanted poster, but hired by the most powerful man in this part of the country to keep the peace. He had asked about him around town and learned nothing negative.

'How did you get your name on a handbill, Nickel?' he asked bluntly. 'You said you were too handy with your gun — you kill someone by accident?'

'Not exactly,' he answered. 'More like I killed him by stupidity. Started out as a silly row when we had both been drinking. You know the bully type, always bumping you with his shoulder when he passed, constantly showing off how tough he is for his friends?' He lifted one shoulder, pausing to take another bite. His expression showed he still regretted the incident. 'Anyway, I'd had a couple drinks one night and, when he ran into me, I shoved him right back. He started to come at me with his fists raised, but I knew he would chew me up like a sugar stick and spit me out. I backed up and put my hand on my gun to warn him off.' He took time to swallow. 'He thought I was making a play and grabbed for his own gun. I was much quicker on the draw, but I was afraid one bullet wouldn't stop a big ape like him, so I shot him three times.'

'I see,' Whitney deduced the circumstances. 'By reaching for your gun to prevent a fist fight, it appeared you tricked him into grabbing his own gun so you could kill him.'

Nickel lowered his head. 'Stupid damn thing to do, Scotty,' he said sadly. 'Kill a man and end up on the run for life because of having a couple drinks.'

'I have a beer on occasion,' Whitney said, 'but I can't see an intelligent use for hard liquor.'

'Makes a person feel bigger, smarter, braver . . . until they act on one of those impulses,' Nickel agreed. 'I haven't had a drink of whiskey since that shooting.'

'Tough lesson to learn,' Whitney sympathized.

'But we were talking about you, Scotty,' the regulator turned back to business. 'You didn't come all this way to take on a babysitting job for a dime-novel scribe. I don't see you being a dangerous killer, but you said you were looking for someone.' He fixed a hard gaze on Whitney. 'I'm asking you to 'fess up as to your purpose, before you end up in a situation like I did. If you kill a man in this town, I need to know the *why* beforehand or you could end up dangling at the end of a noose.'

Whitney decided he would have to trust Nickel. After first getting the regulator's promise to keep the story to himself, he related the attack on his ranch and brought him up to that very point in time.

'If the Polson boys took the herd and continued toward Santa Fe, who tried to kill you?'

'The only thing I can think of is that one of them stayed behind. The stableman said they were going to come back and spend some time here.'

'You said you had never seen them before, so how would they know who you are?'

'That's the puzzle, Nickel — the reason I didn't think the murder of Fancy Dan was meant for me.'

'Does the lady know about your alternative purpose?'

'She does, but she wanted to hire an escort before she entered town.'

'What's her purpose for coming here?' he asked bluntly. 'Did she just want to see a bandit stronghold?'

'She's only looking to write a story,' Whitney lied. He trusted his own fate to Nickel, but he had no right to divulge Amy's true motives. After all, he had promised to keep her secret.

'Hard to believe she doesn't want to write about your quest for justice,' Nickel said.

'I didn't say she wasn't interested,' Whitney admitted. 'She is going to ask Huntley about the Polson boys as part of the payment for my keeping an eye out for her.'

Nickel grinned. 'I thought so.'

'I'll trust you not to say anything about her helping me to your boss. It might give him the wrong idea about her visit.'

He waved a hand to dismiss the

notion. 'Your secret is safe with me, and she won't get anything out of Huntley. He doesn't associate with lowly bandit sorts. He primarily rubs shoulders with the big spenders, those who have class, education or position.'

'Hence the reason he wants to make this some kind of rich man's getaway,' Whitney concluded.

Nickel had finished his meal. He stood up from the table and gave a tip of his head. 'I'll keep an eye out for anyone who might be connected with the Polson brothers.'

'I'm much obliged.'

'Don't you let anyone else get killed on your behalf. Next time, you best be the one in your own bed.'

'I'm not fixing to trade rooms again, but you'll pardon me if I don't get myself shot while sleeping.'

Not bothering to leave payment for his meal, Nickel pivoted from the table and left the diner. The woman waiting tables picked up his empty plate and looked at Whitney.

'Would you like dessert or something else?' she asked.

'No,' he answered. 'Do I owe you for my friend's meal?'

She shook her head. 'My husband and I run this place, but Huntley owns it. We've got over a dozen people who eat for free.'

'Does that include the town doctor?'

'Him and his sweetheart.' She showed a slight smile. 'Kind of a late winter romance, with them both being along in years, but it's kind of cute too.'

'What do I owe you?'

'Six-bits for the house special.'

He placed a silver dollar on the table and rose to his feet. 'You turn out a good meal, ma'am. Thank you.' Touching the brim of his hat he left the café.

Once on to the walk, he decided to head back to the hotel. He needed to be available to speak with Amy and see what she had learned. Her being more of the detective, he would let her point the direction they would go next.

8

J.D. Huntley was extremely entertaining. He had a wit and was as worldly as any man Amy had ever met. He could talk on any subject with a profound intelligence, plus he had interacted with royalty, foreign dignitaries, congressmen and governors. His stories could have filled a dozen of her books.

After an elegant meal, served with a rich red wine and apple-sauce cake, he took her to a nearby closed-up building. It was freshly stained, with wooden floors and a modest window facing the street. Jason opened the door and they went inside. Amy paused to marvel at a stocked bookcase, and there was a large desk, on which sat a typewriter. Against one wall of the room was a massive printing press, along with a small table and several chairs.

'You have a newspaper here?' Amy asked.

He gave her a long stare. 'Not yet. It needs an editor.'

She swallowed and cleared her throat. 'You . . . you're not suggesting that I . . . '

'You're a writer,' he cited the obvious. 'I'll hire someone to operate the press. You can write your books and supervise the writing of our town newspaper.' He spoke quickly, not offering her a chance to reject the idea outright. 'Think of it, Amanda, you would have access to newspapers from all over the country. I subscribe to every important journal and magazine, from medical advances to the *Police Gazette*, the *Saturday Evening Post, Lady's Book*, and can add any other publications of interest. You need only select the articles to reprint. For the local stories, I will give you free rein to write whatever you like. It would be perfect for you, Amanda. You can be a journalist and editor as well as an author of books.'

'You flatter me with such a proposal,

Mr Huntley' — she worded her response carefully — 'but I have a life beyond the walls of this fortress. What you offer is not for me.'

'We could make it work,' he hurried his argument. 'I wouldn't keep you prisoner — you can come and go as you please. I need someone like you, a person of character and prominence. In time, you might consider standing at my side to help rule this bit of paradise.'

'I'm sorry, Jason,' she restated her position. 'It's not for me.'

A hint of panic appeared in the man's eyes, but he quickly masked the emotion. A natural smile came back to his face.

'Before you discount the idea altogether, take a little time and think about it,' he said. 'We have a theater group in town tonight. Let me take you to the performance and explain some other things I have in mind for Little Babylon.'

She opened her mouth to decline, but he held up a hand to stop her. 'You wouldn't rob me of the privilege of sharing an evening with the most desirable woman ever to set foot inside the walls of Little Babylon?'

'You did mention you have had royalty and theater dancers and actresses coming to this place, didn't you?' She smiled. 'I'm sure many of them were superior to me.'

'Beauty is defined by each man's individual appetite, my dear,' he countered.

'That's an insightful adage. I might use it in one of my books.'

'Feel free to do so.'

'I should be getting back to my room,' she said. 'I need to make some notes and jot down some of the wonderful stories you've told me.'

'And tonight?'

'I should like to see the theater group perform, but I prefer not to enter into any sort of courtship. I've told you the truth. I have no intention of staying here after I'm done with my story.'

'Of course,' he dismissed her concern. 'This is only a night at the theater together, a chance for me to pretend I live among a higher social order, rather than being surrounded by bandits and thieves. You will be doing me a great favor.'

She laughed. 'Within those guidelines, I accept.'

* * *

Whitney was lying on his bed when a tap came on the wall. He had heard Amy return, but waited to let her contact him. When he reached the hallway Amy was holding her door open for him. Once inside, they sat down side by side on the bed.

'I wasn't sure you were back at the hotel,' she said. 'I'm glad you have the adjoining room. It makes it easy for us to get together without drawing any unwanted attention.'

'Speaking of unwanted attention, how are you and Huntley doing?'

'He is a charming and unusual man,' Amy admitted. 'He yearns for a social life, but hides away in his residence most of the time. He doesn't associate with most of the average men in Little Babylon,' she added, 'so I don't think I'm going to get any help in finding the Polson brothers unless I come right out and ask for his help.'

'They are not in town, but Nickel is going to keep his eyes open for me,' Whitney said. He took a moment to explain about their conversation.

'Are you sure you can trust him?' Amy asked. 'What if the Polson boys offer him money to join them or stay out of a fight?'

'I believe Nickel is an honest sort,' he said. 'How about your case? You have any luck?'

'Nothing solid I'm afraid. I discovered the doctor visits Huntley every week and takes him a bottle of potassium bromide. I'm not sure what that means, and it might have nothing to do with how Doctor Lyndell came to be here.'

'And how did the doctor end up in Little Babylon?'

Whitney listened to the account of the killing and how the doctor escaped from Colorado Springs. She also told him of the newspaper story and the personal invitation the doctor received. When she finished, Amy added, 'I need to snoop around for some background information about the case, but I don't know how we can do it without going to Colorado Springs.'

'What do you suspect?'

'It strikes me as an odd coincidence that Huntley posts a notice for a doctor and a few weeks later a well-respected doctor is accused of murder. I don't like coincidences and I don't like how the crime was so neatly pinned on Lyndell. I don't see any alternative — I must go back to Colorado Springs and find the answers.'

'There might be another way,' Whitney said. 'My friend, the US Marshal, lives in Colorado Springs. Maybe he could look into the murder for you and get the answers to your questions?'

The option brightened her gloomy

expression. 'Oh, that would be a great help!'

'OK, so what's your idea, Tornado Tess?'

She grinned at his use of her character's name. 'There is a telegraph here in town, but, like everyone else, the man works for Huntley. If I start asking serious questions with my inquiries, we'll both be treading on thin ice.'

'I learned Morse code after we moved to the ranch,' Whitney informed her. 'The telegraph line was only a mile from our house — it ran to a nearby fort and also to a couple of towns some miles away. Anyhow, I had my own telegraph key and receiver until the house was burned down. I used to ride over to the line so I could tap in and order supplies from Raton. On occasion I would contact Colorado Springs or some other nearby town to set up a sale or meet with a buyer.'

'Scotty, you never cease to amaze me!' Amy exclaimed. 'If you could find a way to send the message yourself, it would save us — *me* — that horribly long trip back and forth.'

'Make a list of the information you need and I'll work something out.'

'What if you get caught?'

'I'll wait until the place is locked up for the night and find a way to do the job.'

'There's a theater group in town tonight,' she said, thinking quickly. 'There's a good chance the operator will go to the show.'

'That would allow me to slip in and send the message.'

'What about the answer?'

'If it's something he can't put on the wire, I'll have him send it by mail. It only takes a couple days by stage and a letter won't look suspicious, because I'm checking on the Polson boys. Nickel already knows about them.'

'It's a sensational plan!' she declared happily. 'Scotty, you're the best partner I could have every asked for!' Amy threw her arms around his neck and hugged him tightly.

Whitney knew her jubilation was due to his helping her to live out her dream. She was becoming Tornado Tess, acting the part of a detective, possibly working on a scheme to clear a good man's name. He should have gone along with it, hugged her back and maintained his self-control.

But when she broke from the clinch, she paused, inches away, a wonderfully dreamy expression on her face as she gazed right into his eyes. He threw caution and good sense to the wind and kissed her inviting lips!

Amy didn't react immediately, seeming to accept the advance and allowing him to linger a full two or three seconds. Then she drew her hands in from the embrace and pressed lightly against his chest.

Common sense flooded his fevered brain. Whitney broke off the kiss and leapt to his feet. 'Damn,' he muttered huskily, 'I didn't mean to do that.'

Amy appeared baffled as well, refusing to look up at him. 'Yes, well, um, I'll write down the information I need from your friend and give it to you.'

'Yeah,' he replied, battling a raging inner turmoil over losing control. He hated the idea that Amy would think he had taken advantage of the moment — which he had!

'I'll be next door,' he said softly, backing away from her. 'Just tap on the wall when you want me.'

'All right,' she murmured, still hiding her eyes beneath veiled lids and long lashes.

Whitney made a swift exit without a backward glance. When he entered his room next door, he had to resist the urge to pound his fist against the wall . . . Amy would have heard it! He crossed to the street and stared out the window unseeing. His conscience was beating him over the head with a double jackhammer.

What the hell got into you? he demanded to know. *Have you lost your senses?*

While he hadn't been around that

many alluring women, he had always been courteous and polite. Somehow, holding Amy close and looking into her enchanting eyes, he had been overwhelmed with desire and lost control of both body and mind.

Smart move, you clumsy ox! She'll never trust giving you another hug!

★   ★   ★

To try and summon a measure of composure and reasoning, Amy took out her notepad. She tore out a page so she could write down what she needed to say to Whitney's contact. When she put the pencil to the paper her brain refused to concentrate on Doctor Lyndell or the case at hand. She sighed with exasperation, set aside the blank paper and looked at the last paragraph of her story.

The words were a blur. It was impossible to concentrate on anything except Whitney's uncharacteristic behavior. Always the perfect gentleman, he had done little more than tease her previously — although his taunting could occasionally have been construed as light-hearted romance. He had taken her arm on the stairway and also when they crossed the street or when rowdy men were nearby. The actions were purely protective gestures — so she had assumed.

In the story she was now writing, Tess was very taken with her lead man . . . a man very much like Whitney. It caused her to wonder if she and Tess were each progressing toward a mutual identity. Tess had always been the side of Amy she kept hidden, bold, courageous and utterly comfortable around men. As for her love life, Tess had experienced romantic encounters which far exceeded the few moments Amy had actually shared with a man. The kiss from Whitney was only the third time she had ever been kissed . . . and one of those had been a dare when she was fourteen!

Unable to concentrate on the case, she decided to jot a few lines of her story.

The words came so fast she could barely write them down. Emotions were the key ingredient to driving a story — hate, sorrow, lust, love, anger, joy — and she was flooded with all manner of heightened sensations. It took only a few minutes to complete several pages describing a torrid encounter between Tess and the love interest in her new story, Flash McCord.

Pausing to reread what she had written, Amy was thrilled at the flow of sensuous feelings and full blown passion shared between the characters. If this were an underground book, one of those forbidden novels a bookseller keeps behind the counter, she might have added even more risqué details. Her books never went beyond a kiss, but these two characters could have easily expanded her principles and ended up . . .

'Whoa, Tess!' she said aloud, alarmed at the thought. 'Whatever are you thinking!'

★　★　★

The afternoon sun came through the window at just the right angle to hit the room's only mirror. Because of his rash behavior, Whitney vowed to look his best for the next meeting with Amy. He would apologize and reassure her he was indeed a gentleman. The kiss had been a one-time slip. It would not happen again.

Unable to see his reflection in the glare of light, he moved the washstand over in front of the entrance, set the mirror on it and leaned it against the door. Then he backed up so he could see himself. He adjusted the string tie and eyed his new suit with a critical inspection. His boots were polished and his hat was dusted off and reasonably clean. As for wearing the gun belt and gun, he could always —

The mirror shattered — simultaneously with the blast from a rifle!

Whitney instinctively ducked, spinning around and drawing his pistol at the same time. He scooted over to the wall and carefully peered around the open curtain. The shop across the way was the bakery. It was only a single-story building, so someone must have taken a shot at him from the roof.

There came a pounding on the wall. A few seconds later and the door was yanked open, spilling the remainder of the broken mirror on to the floor. Amy was in the hallway. She swept the room at a glance and regarded him with a combined look of fright and confusion.

'Were you practicing your draw? Did your gun go off by accident?' She asked the questions rapidly, out of breath from her scare and having rushed to his room.

Whitney holstered his gun. 'Someone mistook the mirror for me.' He grunted. 'Guess that buries any notion that Fancy Dan was the man the killer wanted.'

'But you said the Polson boys were not in town!'

Whitney stepped over and moved the washstand table out of the way. He was beginning to pick up the pieces from the broken mirror when Henry and Nickel appeared.

'What the hell, honcho?' Nickel complained, stopping in the doorway. 'Do I have to keep an eye on you every minute?'

'I believe the shooter was on the roof of the bakery, Nickel. Had I been looking out the window, he would have sure enough put a round through my gullet.'

'You had best keep the curtain drawn and not use the lamp after dark,' the regulator warned. 'Whoever is after you is damn serious about getting the job done.'

'I'll be adding the price of that mirror to your stay, Scotty,' Henry snapped off the words seriously, but he had a look a concern on his face. 'I'll bring up a spare I keep in the back room, but don't be leaving it out for any more shooting practice.'

'Yeah, I'll be careful.'

Nickel walked over and glanced out the window. Seeing nothing suspicious, he looked back at Whitney. 'You sure you told me the truth, Scotty? No one knows you are here?'

'I swear to you, I haven't seen a single face I recognize.'

'I'll have a look around over at the bakery and see if anyone saw whoever pulled the trigger. It's likely a waste of time, but it'll make me feel like I'm doing my job.'

'Catching the shooter would make me feel a whole lot better.'

The two men left and Whitney picked up the rest of the broken glass. He finished and turned around to discover Amy had not left. She started to step into the room, but he stopped her.

'No! Don't!' he said abruptly.

She flinched at his tone, but held her chin up in defiance. 'I'm not afraid of you because of . . . of what happened in my room. I know you wouldn't physically force your attentions on me.'

He had to grin at her statement. 'It's not that,' he explained. 'I don't want you stepping on a piece of broken glass.' He tipped his head down at her bare feet.

'Oh,' she gulped. The realization of his warning caused a crimson flush to rise in her cheeks. 'I didn't think about not having on any shoes.'

'But you're right,' he returned to her concern. 'I won't let my heart overrule my head again. You have my word.'

'I . . . it wasn't all your fault,' she murmured in little more than a whisper. 'I shouldn't have . . . I didn't . . . '

'It's for me to apologize,' Whitney stopped her agonizing. 'You gave me a brotherly hug and I took advantage of it. I'm sorry.'

'You should leave town,' she warned. 'Someone has tried to kill you twice and you don't even know who it is. What's to stop him from walking right up to you and sticking a knife between your ribs?'

'You make a good point,' he said. 'Maybe I would recognize him, but just haven't seen him yet.'

'What do you mean?'

'The first attempt was at night in a darkened room. The man didn't risk a match or light to make sure of his target. This second attempt was an ambush from across the street.'

'So?'

'Think like your detective, Tornado Tess,' he advised her. 'Both times the killer was careful not to show himself. You said it yourself, if there was no chance I would recognize him, he could have walked right up to me and either stabbed or shot me.'

'I see what you mean, Scotty, but you've been snooping around town. How come you haven't seen anyone you recognized?'

'Because I've been out in the open. I've been looking for several men I've never met. This guy must have seen me and has been careful to stay hidden. It means I'll have to figure a way to draw him out into the open.'

'And how will you do that?'

'One problem at a time,' he told her.

'First we have to send off your telegraph message. Do you have it written down?'

'Yes, we can go over it whenever you're ready.'

'Tornado Tess is on the job,' he quipped. The comment invoked a brightness in Amy's face and her eyes positively sparkled. Whitney felt a huge relief. She had obviously forgiven his impetuous kiss. 'As soon as I finish cleaning up this glass and Henry brings a replacement mirror, I'll be along.'

Amy didn't reply again, making her way back into her own room. Whitney went to the window and closed the curtains. He would heed Nickel's advice: no lights to cast his silhouette and no standing in front of open windows.

9

The telegrapher also handled the mail for Huntley. He was an elderly gent — one suspected of passing counterfeit money — who had found a safe haven at Little Babylon to escape prosecution. He had a room in the back of the tiny office, but left for the evening performance at the large casino — it boasted a room with a curtained stage.

Being watchful for ambush, Whitney had gone out the back way of the hotel, circled the stables and worked his way through the alleyways and behind buildings. He was certain no one had followed by the time he saw the postman-telegrapher leave his office. The entrance was no problem as the man had left his windows open to cool his bedroom.

Whitney slipped inside and went to the front office. He discovered the mail was behind a locked cage, but the telegraph was at a desk, with paper and pen handy. Obviously the operator felt there was no need to lock away something no one was likely to steal. It took only a few minutes to complete his chore, then he made his exit back the way he had come.

Rather than return to the hotel, he worked the shadows and peeked into the saloons and eateries. He had about decided it was a waste of time when he looked through a front window into the Mexican tavern and spied a familiar-looking face!

Raw undiluted rage swept over Whitney, penetrating him to the bone like a sudden blast of wind from an arctic winter storm. He took several steps toward the entrance, but his good sense screamed at him to wait. He didn't want to start a fight in a crowded café and maybe hurt innocent people. With his jaw anchored so tightly his teeth ached, he backed into the shadows and waited for the man to come out.

Not five minutes later a figure approached out of the darkness. It was Nickel.

'What the hell, Scotty?' he asked, stopping next to him. 'Two of my guards reported you were sneaking around in the dark like an alley cat. What are you up to?'

'I know who killed Dan,' he told him. 'And I know who betrayed me and my brother.'

Nickel gave him a serious look. 'For what he did to you, I'll grant you deserve some payback, but no one gets away with cold-blooded murder in this town. If he killed Fancy Dan, he will swing from a rope.'

Whitney spun on Nickel — he thought to argue the point — but a gun magically appeared in the man's hand. He stopped in mid-breath, staring at the muzzle of Nikel's .44.

'Damn, Nickel,' he said, shaking his head in awe, 'You move quicker than a scorched bobcat. I didn't even see you reach for your gun! Were you born with a pistol in each hand?'

'I told you I was too handy with a gun for my own good. You don't want to cross me.'

'Crossing you is the last thing I want to do,' Whitney replied. 'I wasn't intending to fight you over this.'

'Just argue your right to apprehend this guy yourself.'

'Something like that.'

Nickel reached over and removed Whitney's Frontier Colt. 'You make the arrest. No guns,' he stated, shoving Whitney's pistol into his belt, 'And the man has to be able to walk to the gallows.'

Whitney had no time to debate. The door to the cantina opened and out walked his prey. He swiftly stepped over to block the way as Nickel moved in with his gun still drawn.

'Milt Dewey!' Whitney snarled the name of his missing hired hand. 'You double-crossing, dirty, stinking, murdering sack of rat guts!'

Milt instantly paled. His hand dropped

to his gun, but Nickel had him covered. 'I wouldn't!' he warned him, moving in to take Dewey's gun. He backed up and announced, 'You're under arrest for the murder of Fancy Dan and the attempted murder of Scotty here.' Nickel flashed a wry simper. 'Soon as you two finish discussing old times, you're going to jail.'

'There wasn't supposed to be any killin',' Milt cried. 'Tom said we would only steal the horses. I didn't have nothing to do with your brother and the others being — '

But the punch to his face cut off the words. Milt reeled back against the side of the building. Before he could gather his senses, Whitney hammered him several more times.

Milt was no wilted rose when it came to mixing it up. He battled back, catching Whitney with a hard shot above the eye and again on the side of the face. He charged into Whitney and they landed in the middle of the street.

Rolling about, Milt kicked, gouged,

and even bit Whitney on the forearm; he scrapped like a cornered animal. A crowd gathered, as the performance at the casino had ended and there were a great many people on the street.

Whitney didn't intend to lose an eye or get his nose or ear bitten off. He pulled up his right foot, wedged it against Milt's stomach and shoved him away. Before the man could grab hold of him again Whitney scrambled to his feet. He was ready when Milt waded in a second time. Blocking a roundhouse right, he launched a punishing attack of lefts and rights. He smashed the man's lips with granite knuckles and closed his left eye. When Milt lunged at him, trying to tackle him, Whitney leapt to the side and clubbed him viciously on the back of the neck. The blow sent him sprawling on to his face.

Twice more Milt got his feet under him and twice more Whitney pounded him decisively to the ground. The vision of his hired hands, of the widow smoldering and burning, of his brother dying in his arms — it drove him to vent his rage and grief. Milt went down for the last time and lay gasping for air, his face and shirt bloody, beaten until he was not fully conscious.

'Leave enough for us to hang,' Nickel spoke up, moving into the circle the crowd had formed. He stuck Whitney's gun back into his holster and chuckled. 'Wouldn't want anyone to say we regulators didn't treat our prisoners with compassion and benevolence.'

Whitney's chest heaved from the physical exertion as he sucked wind for his lungs. He had the taste of blood in his mouth and a second trickle seeped into one eye. Without a word he turned for the nearest watering trough. The spectators parted a path and began to break up. He heard words like *brutal, vicious, merciless* — each attached to the term *beating*. He hadn't known he was capable of such savage fury. He removed his hat, dropped to his knees and submerged his head under the cool water for a few seconds. Rising up, he shook the water from his hair and wiped it from his eyes.

'S-Scotty?'

He recognized Amy's voice and groaned. 'I didn't want you to see that,' he said tightly, lowering his head, while his shoulders drooped from shame.

'Are you all right?'

Whitney rinsed off his hands to remove the blood. He suddenly felt dirty, conscience-stricken over the desire to beat a man to death with his bare hands. He turned slowly, fearful to see a look of horror and disgust on Amy's face. After watching him act the part of an enraged animal, it was to be expected.

However, Amy's expression showed only concern. She moved in closely and examined his face, lifting a hand to finger a bruise gingerly and a cut above his eye.

'We need to bandage that,' she said, referring to the latter. 'What about your ribs? I saw him kick you when you were fighting on the ground.'

'I'm fine,' he told her. Unable to

meet her worried scrutiny, he added, 'I'm right sorry you saw me . . . like that.'

'Jason asked Nickel what the fight was about,' she gave him the details. 'He said that man is the one who helped kill your brother and the others.'

'Yes, the missing hired hand. I felt bad, thinking he had been left wounded or dead out in the hills. I searched for him for most of the day, before I even stopped to bury my brother and the others.'

'I'm glad you won the fight,' Amy said.

He took a moment to study her. 'You ought to be shocked or sickened at watching me lose control like that. I might have beaten him to death.'

Strangely, a pert smile curled her lips. 'I've seen you lose control before . . . like when you kissed me.'

Whitney laughed at the comparison. 'If it isn't too impolite to say so, I definitely prefer the kiss.'

'Me too,' she replied.

Stunned at her bluntness, he was prevented from following up on her startling admission because of Huntley's approach.

'Nickel informs me that Milt Dewey is a man you've been looking for.'

'When the Polson brothers burned my ranch to the ground and stole our herd of horses, I thought he had been killed by the rustlers. It turns out he was working with them.'

'We'll have a hearing for him in the morning and hang him tomorrow afternoon.'

'Justice is swift in Little Babylon,' Whitney said.

'Controlling a town with a wide range of dignitaries and desperadoes, it is necessary to act decisively on these matters. It sets a precedent for everyone else.'

'Do you need me to tell what I know about Milt?'

'Not at all,' Huntley replied. 'Nickel said he confessed to killing Dan and also taking a shot at you. If you wish to attend the hanging, it will be at the livery.' He shrugged his shoulders. 'There isn't a decent tree for fifty miles around and we never wasted the time to build a gallows.'

'I reckon a block and tackle will get the job done all the same.'

Huntley gave him a nod, then turned to Amy. 'Would you allow me to see you back to your room?'

'Thank you, Jason, but I'll go with Scotty. I need to tend to the cut above his eye.'

'I could summon the town doctor?' he offered.

'He will likely need to attend to your prisoner,' she said, declining the offer. 'Thank you for a wonderful evening.'

'Keep my offer in mind, Amanda,' he said smoothly. 'You would be a great addition to this town.'

Amy waited until he was out of earshot before she leaned close and spoke to Whitney in a hushed voice. 'Were you able to send the message?'

'Yes, exactly what you wrote down.

The marshal should get it tomorrow, if he is in town. We should get an answer back in a couple days by stage or wire, depending on what he has to tell us.'

They reached Amy's room and she used some water and a damp cloth to clean Whitney's abrasions. She decided the cut over his eye was not as bad as it had looked, so there was no need to try to apply a bandage. Finally, she began to use a damp cloth to remove the blood gently from the scrapes on his knuckles.

'You needn't fuss with my hands, Miss Cole. I can do that myself,' Whitney told her quietly.

She paused, holding his right hand between her own, and looked up at him. 'I never thought about a man breaking his knuckles or cutting them on another man's teeth before. I . . . I write fight scenes in my books but my hero never gets hurt.'

'Guess I'm not of the same caliber as Trapper Joe.'

'No, you're not.' Whitney thought she

had insulted him, but she lowered her eyelids to shield her eyes. 'You're a caring, feeling, human being. Trapper Joe is an imaginary character, one I control through my writing. You have honest emotions, you are a caring, decent man, but you get mad, you lose control, you are real.'

He countered with, 'I would think you'd prefer Joe to a regular guy. He will always do what you expect and won't disappoint you like an ordinary man.'

She lifted her gaze. He thought for a moment she was going to say something back along the same line of thought, but she turned the wagon in a new direction.

'Jason wants me to start up a town newspaper. He said I can write all the stories I want and he will see they get published.' She shrugged. 'He knows a lot of people in high places.'

'That would be the offer he was talking about,' Whitney presumed, remembering Jason's parting words. 'Are you thinking of staying?'

'I told him no, but he makes a tempting proposition. I would have at least two people working for me — a press operator and another writer. He would provide me with a residence and housekeeper, and I would have anything I wanted for free. Once the train spur is complete, he said I would have access to travel anywhere in the world.'

'Sounds impressive,' Whitney said, not the least bit happy at the idea. He tried to conceal a sudden flare-up of emotions when he expounded on the offer. 'Reckon Huntley also has an interest in more than your literary skills.'

'Yes, I'm certain he intends we should have a more amicable relationship. He mentioned that he would like to make me his queen.'

'He has a status in life few men can match — seems a charming sort too.'

'Very,' she concurred. 'I've never met anyone as worldly as Jason. He keeps abreast of everything that's going on, whether it's in our country or on another continent. You ought to see his collection of books and magazines.'

'Tough for an ordinary fellow to compete against all he has to offer,' Whitney said thickly. Pulling his hand away, he rose up from the bed. 'I'll be saying good night to you, Miss Cole.'

She seemed surprised at his abruptness. 'Of course, Scotty, I'm sure you must ache all over from the fight. I'll see you in the morning.'

Whitney didn't know why, but he had to get out of Amy's room. He couldn't listen to her brag about some gent who wanted to make her his queen, while being close enough to hold her tight and taste her sweet lips — damn! His gut felt like he had swallowed a handful of nails. What was that all about?

★　★　★

Amy was confused by Whitney's unexpected departure. Writing as Tornado Tess, she had administered treatment to a number of men and every one of them reacted with a fond appreciation. Playing nurse was supposed to endear a woman to a man, yet Whitney had suddenly become sober and curt. He didn't follow the script worth a hoot.

Reviewing the conversation, she recalled his mood had changed when the subject turned to Huntley. She was struck by a glimmer of understanding. Whitney was jealous!

The realization caused a mixture of emotions. He had no right to be jealous, because they had never held hands — except for while she treated his bruised knuckles — or done any courting. In fact, the single time he kissed her had been wholly impulsive. She hadn't been given the chance either to return the kiss or slap his face. The memory caused her to speculate about what she would have done.

If, instead of a quick withdrawal and hasty exit, he had declared his undying affection for her, would she have ended up kissing him a second time? Did she even know how she felt about him?

And what about Jason Huntley? He wished to court and woo her until she accepted his propositions. She would be an editor of a newsletter, while continuing to write books. He offered her a place to live, but she knew it was a prelude to making her his wife. Is that something she wanted? Was she of a mind to consider it?

Amy picked up her notebook and began to scribble. Flash McCord was not as uncooperative as Whitney Scott. She had anticipated he might want to thank her with a kiss — at least attempt one! Well, Flash McCord would do exactly what Tornado Tess wanted. And their second kiss would put a permanent curl in his toes!

10

Amy spent the next morning visiting with Belva and Ralph. They stopped once for a customer, but it was a slow morning. It didn't take long before she decided the doctor was not the sort to kill anyone. He struck her as a caring and gentle man, soft-spoken, with a subtle wit. Conscientious to a fault, he was genuinely concerned for some of the injuries Milt Dewey had suffered in his fight with Whitney. He worried the man wouldn't be able to eat properly without the use of several of his teeth. Amy pointed out that the man was due to be hanged for murdering Fancy Dan, but Ralph still fretted that he should have done more to help him.

She did double-check the account of how he came to be in Little Babylon. Belva had covered the incident in detail and his story was much the same. He hadn't seen or spoken to the witness and he had no idea who might have shot his patient's husband.

'And the woman was unconscious throughout the entire episode?' Amy asked him at last. At his nod, she also asked, 'How bad were her injuries?'

'Not life-threatening, but I didn't get a lot of time to look over her bruises. When the man was shot, I turned my attention to him. The policeman entered seconds after the shooting. I barely had time to assess it to be a mortal wound.'

'When did the woman regain consciousness?'

'She came to a few minutes after the policeman arrived. She was both alarmed and shocked to discover her husband had been shot.'

'Is there anything else you can tell me about the woman or her relationship with her husband?' Amy asked.

'The policeman told me he had warned Lyle Carter, the husband, before, but a woman can't press charges against her husband. And there are few judges who will put a man behind bars for striking his wife. Policeman Lowe said he understood why I had shot the man. He was quite sympathetic about the whole affair.'

'You don't believe he could have done the shooting?'

'Heavens no,' Ralph replied. 'He was a block away when the shot was fired.'

'Do you think your friend can help us?' Belva finally broke her long silence. 'We are treated very well here, but we are still prisoners. Until Ralph can show his face outside these gates, we will never be truly free.'

'Scotty contacted his friend in Colorado Springs and asked him to look into your situation. We should hear something back in a few days. I hope the information he provides will help us solve this mystery.'

'The investigation turned up only me as the suspect,' Ralph said. 'No one saw anyone else near the house or window. I'm certain I would have been convicted if I had shown up for the hearing.'

'So you ran.'

'Right or wrong, I didn't want to spend my life treating other prisoners at Canyon City.'

Belva spoke up again. 'I don't see how you expect to discover who shot Lyle Carter from a hundred miles away.'

Amy displayed a satisfied simper and explained, 'Scotty's contact is a US Marshal.'

The news impressed both of them. Belva took the doctor's hand and squeezed it. 'You see, darling? I knew Tess would help us.'

'Only if the marshal finds something,' he maintained his doubts.

'It's all about discovering the motive,' she said. 'If we can learn why someone wanted Lyle dead, we are halfway to knowing who killed him.'

Ralph glanced at the clock on the wall. 'It's time I went over to visit Mr Huntley.' He walked over and picked up his bag. He paused before leaving and smiled at Amy.

'For what you are trying to do, Belva

and I will be eternally grateful. But if you can't find a motive or killer, don't fret on it. As long as we have one another, we'll get by.'

'That's very sweet.'

'No,' Belva piped up, 'sweet is him finally asking me to marry him.'

Ralph laughed. 'Yes, I've only loved her since we first met. Took me all this time to get around to asking her.'

A customer entered as Ralph was leaving so Amy said goodbye to Belva. She found Whitney standing near the alleyway waiting. She paused to take notice of several people, all wandering in the same direction, headed for the livery.

'Is it time?' she asked, meaningfully.

'An hour or so yet, but I suspect they want to have a good place to watch the hanging.'

'I'll understand if you want to go, but I think I will pass.'

Whitney gave a negative shake of his head. 'I worked off the steam I had built up last night. Justice will be served when Milt is hanged, but it's not something I have to see.'

She eyed him thoughtfully. 'You continue to surprise me, Scotty.'

'In spite of how it might have looked during the fight, I'm not a violent man. It was more having Milt betray our trust. He sold us out, a man who had worked alongside of us for nearly two years. He helped the Polson brothers kill the men he had lived with — played cards and laughed and joked with. He watched as those butchers shot the widow who did the cooking and set fire to the house with her and my brother still inside.'

'And after all that, you have no wish to watch him hang?'

'If he was to grab a gun and make a break, I would shoot him down like a rabid dog. But I'm not keen on watching anyone hang. He dies for the sake of justice here in Babylon, because he took another man's life and tried to kill me. When he hits the end of the rope his debt for all he did to me will be square.'

⋆ ⋆ ⋆

That evening, Huntley shared a private dinner with Amy at his special table in the Refectory. When they had finished, he took hold of her arm and escorted her out the back way.

'I came across something I would like to show you,' he said. 'It will only take a few minutes, but I know you'll be delighted.'

Amy went along with him, but her heart began to pound with anticipation. Huntley had been a perfect host, but he did control everything inside the walls of Little Babylon. What if he had something romantic planned? How would he handle rejection? If he decided to make her his concubine, his prisoner, who would stop him?

She shook the ridiculous notions from her head. Huntley thrived on proprieties and gentlemanly comportment. He was not the type to force his attentions on a woman or keep her as an unwilling captive.

The bald man, who always seemed to be nearby, was at the door to Huntley's office. He had a worried frown on his face.

'You sure?' are the only two words he uttered.

'Thank you, Bruno, but you can go ahead and get your supper. We'll only be a few minutes.'

He showed reluctance but shuffled away.

Huntley leaned close and whispered to Amy. 'The man is as loyal as any hound, but he can sometimes be a burden.'

'He certainly does worry about your safety. Wherever did you find him?'

'I saved him from being hanged,' he explained. 'Cost me a thousand dollars, but he has been my faithful guardian ever since.'

'So what did you have to show me?'

Huntley opened the door to his office apartment. She took a moment and marveled at his good taste in furniture and décor. A mild sense of relief coursed through her when she noticed the door to what was probably the bedroom was closed.

Huntley pulled the door shut behind them and led the way to his desk. There were three books laid out for display, brand new from outward appearance, and he stopped to show them to her.

'These are copies from each first printing,' he stated proudly, 'signed by the author herself. *Little Women, Good Wives* and *Little Men*, all written by Louisa May Alcott.'

Amy gaped. She had read Little Women years ago, but never got around to the sequels. She reached out and touched the books as delicately as if they were made of flower petals.

'How did you ever manage this?'

'I have many friends in all sorts of places,' he replied. 'It's an example of what I've been telling you. If you cast your lot with me, I have enough money and personal contacts to make all of your dreams come true.'

'About your money . . .'

'I didn't steal it,' he said at once, deadly serious. 'It happens that a group of Frenchmen wanted to help the South win the war against the Union. They sent gold over via a special envoy to support the cause — believing they would be paid back with the title to millions of acres of land when the South won the war. As it turned out, the envoy ran into a band of Comanche, who really didn't care who won the war. The Indians slaughtered them to the last man and took all of the horses and supplies. The gold was in bricks, so they didn't even bother with it. I happened on to the scene after the Indians had gone.' He shrugged. 'The rest of the story is written in the history of Little Babylon. I have a fortune in several different banks and this town is paying handsome dividends. You see now why I can boast — whatever you can dream of, you can have.'

'Why stay here? Why not move to a big city and do something more with so much money?'

'Because I suffer from a minor health problem. It does not affect me here, but I would not fare well at business meetings or social functions where I don't have total control. Besides which, I rather like being a king.' He paused to flash an engaging grin. 'All I need is a queen to make my life complete.'

Huntley moved in closer to her. The desire was bright in his eyes as he reached out and took hold of her hands. 'Dear Amanda,' he said softly, passionately, 'stay with me. Let me prove to you that I am worthy of a woman like you.'

'Jason,' she murmured, shielding her apprehension, 'I wish . . . '

'I've been truthful and straightforward with you, Amanda,' he continued to press for acceptance. 'We don't have to live here — I can take you any place in the world. I can give you anything you want.'

She pulled back. 'I'm happy with the life I have, Jason.'

'But I would live only to serve your

every whim.' He was growing more desperate. 'Give me a chance. I know you could learn to love me!'

In equal desperation to end the one-sided devotion, she blurted out, 'I can't love you, Jason! I already love another man!'

The words stopped him like a dousing with icy water. His head moved slowly from side to side. 'You . . . love another man?' He appeared both crushed and incredulous, letting go of her hands and taking a step back. 'But you came to Little Babylon alone. What man would allow a woman like you to travel all this way unescorted?'

'Scotty is my escort.'

'Yes, but — ' He stopped speaking and began to rub his temples, as if suffering a sudden headache. 'You said you met him on the way. You said . . . ' But he didn't continue.

Amy felt sorrow and compassion at the same time. She had told him at the beginning that she wanted no more than friendship. She had kept him at a distance and done nothing to let him think she had changed her position. Even so, it was difficult to squash the hopes of such a charismatic, enamored suitor.

A flush suddenly came into Jason's complexion, his features contorted and his eyes showed an odd sort of dissociative fear. He grew rigid, uttered a 'No!' and staggered toward the door to his bedroom.

Amy rushed to put a supportive arm about him, or he would have fallen. The two of them crashed into his room and he landed on the bed. He began to thrash about, his face blank and his eyes fixed sightlessly. Even as she worked to keep him on the bed, his entire body began to tremble and shake.

She had suspected his health problem might be something like this. Having seen epileptic fits before, she knew the only thing she could do was keep him from swallowing his tongue or hurting himself. She stripped off his belt and forced it between his teeth, while trying to pin him down on the bed. His arm jerked about, his hand caught hold of her bodice and he about knocked her to the floor. Battling to control his flailing arms she hoped this would be a short seizure.

★   ★   ★

The town runner gave the telegram to Whitney. He couldn't imagine how the marshal could have gotten the information together so quickly. When he read the few lines, everything fell into place.

He went first to the fancy eatery, but the drapes were pulled back and Huntley's reserved table was being cleared away. The man had obviously taken Amy to his office apartment. He saw the brute, Huntley's bodyguard, entering a nearby tavern. That meant he wouldn't be around to stop Whitney from going to see the two of them. And this was as good a time as any. The three of them could sort this out together and see what the king of Little Babylon wanted to do.

Whitney went down the alley to the side entrance, the one he knew was used by Huntley, and hurried up the stairs. He paused to knock but no one answered. When he pushed open the door, he heard noise coming from the bedroom — it sounded like sobbing!

Whitney raced across the office, but slid to a screeching halt before he reached the bedroom door. Amy appeared at the entrance, her hair disheveled, her face flushed and she was busy trying to tuck in her blouse — which had been torn open to the waist! He stood dumbstruck and immobile, right up until she saw him.

'Scotty!' she cried, instantly pulling the torn remnants of her blouse together. 'What are you doing here?'

'Miss Cole,' he bit off the words like chips of ice. 'I apologize for interrupting. I didn't know you were . . . privately engaged.'

'Amanda!' Huntley called from within

the dark room behind her. 'What did you do with my belt? I need it to hold up my trousers!'

She appeared confused, tongue-tied and Huntley's plea caused her cheeks to glow red with embarrassment.

'You go ahead and finish whatever it is you were doing,' he said tightly, whirling back around toward the exit. 'What I had to say can wait until morning.'

'Scotty!' she gasped. 'This isn't what you think!' But Whitney was already out the door.

11

Amy wanted to go after Whitney, but Huntley followed after her, holding up his pants with one hand. He caught up with her before she had a chance to leave.

'I'm so sorry you had to witness my . . . special kind of misery,' he said. 'I've been taking medication that staves off the dreaded episodes, but . . . well, I'm afraid getting over-emotional can set off an attack.'

'The medication is potassium bromide . . . I know.'

'You know?' he was perplcxcd. 'How could you possibly — ?'

'I had a girlfriend who suffered from the same affliction, but they didn't have any medicine for it back then.'

'Yes, it helps, but it is not a cure,' he explained. 'Doctor Lyndell has me on a tonic of sorts, but it can only do so much.' He let out a deep sigh. 'I fear I will suffer the torture of the disease all my life.'

'A great many people have had epilepsy — Julius Caesar, a great czar of Russia, even Lord Byron, who is such a fine poet. It is not something to be ashamed of.'

'They don't call them fits for nothing,' he lamented. 'Very little warning and never a memory of what happened. It is a despicable ailment and a fit destroys a person's self-worth.'

'I believe the more educated doctors refer to them as seizures, rather than fits these days. And I didn't abandon my friend because she suffered from epilepsy. I know it isn't a form of being crazy or something.'

'You saw me at my worst.'

'And it makes no difference to how I feel, Jason,' she responded. 'I like you very much . . . as a friend. You're handsome, charming and very knowledgeable. If I wasn't already in love with another man, I could easily fall in love with you.'

'I would like for you to have the books,' he said, indicating the three lying on the desk. 'They were a gift of appreciation from an elderly lady who had the habit of wedding rich men. Two of them died under mysterious circumstances.' He smiled. 'In truth, I don't think she wanted to pack them all the way to Europe.'

'I shall cherish them, Jason.'

'Is there any way I can persuade you to stay?' he queried. 'Little Babylon would certainly benefit from a newspaper.'

'I'm sorry, but I have other plans.'

'Well, if you have need of anything while you're here, you only have to ask.'

Amy moved over and kissed him on the cheek. 'Thank you, Jason. That means a lot.'

★ ★ ★

Whitney had intended to get himself a beer. In his present mood, a couple of hard drinks might have been more appropriate. He hated to admit it, but he felt like getting so drunk he couldn't think or feel. It hurt inside until his teeth ached.

'There you are, Scotty!' Nickel came out of the darkness to stop him on the street. 'Been looking for you.'

'What for?'

'They are at the gate,' he informed him. 'The Polson boys and two hired guns just arrived.'

Whitney's hand went down and gripped his pistol butt. The pain inside suddenly had a release — fury, and the desire to extract vengeance. 'They're at the gate?'

'You can't take on all five by yourself, my justice-minded friend. Even I wouldn't go up against that many alone.'

'I can't let them get away and I don't know if an arrest would stick. With Milt dead, I don't have anyone to testify against them.'

Cyrus came sauntering down the main avenue to join the two of them.

'Them fellers are getting real antsy, Nick. What are we going to do with them?'

'Scotty and I were just discussing the odds.'

Cyrus snorted his skepticism. 'Two of you against five? Them numbers don't work out even.'

'You got a better idea in mind?' Nickel asked him. 'You think maybe we can talk them into taking us on one or two at a time?'

'Hey, this isn't your fight!' Whitney protested. 'I don't want you getting yourself killed on my account.'

'You helped me arrest Milt,' Nickel argued. 'It's only fair I lend a hand.'

'Well, ain't neither of you quick enough to take three of those polecats,' Cyrus said. 'If you're hell-bent on trying this, I'll take the odd man. That way you only have two each.'

'Damn, Cyrus, I can't let you do that,' Nickel said.

'I told you when I hired on, Nick, I'm loyal to the brand . . . whether it's cattle or a town or a good man like Mr Huntley. I do what's needed, even when I'm not asked or given the order.'

'I'll grant you're the most faithful man I ever met,' Nickel agreed.

'So, we going to do this?' Cyrus asked.

'I don't know,' Whitney held back. 'I'd feel lower than dirt if I was to get you both killed.'

'You don't have a say any more,' Nickel vowed. 'I'll take 'em by myself — me and Cyrus — if you don't want to come along.'

'I'm a fair shot, but I've never killed a man in a gunfight,' Whitney admitted.

Nickel laughed. 'I'll bet you that pack of coyotes has never stood up to a fair fight before either.'

'Fair?' Whitney's voice raised an octave. 'You think five against three is a fair fight?'

'Come on,' Cyrus was grinning. 'It'll be fun.'

Whitney gave a hard look at Cyrus. 'You are a strange man.'

'You can buy him a drink when this is over, he'll be your friend for life,' Nickel joked. 'Let's get going before those boys have a chance to escape.'

★ ★ ★

Amy was reaching for the door to leave when Bruno burst into the room. He nearly knocked the books out of her arms before he skidded to a halt.

'Sorry,' he grunted.

'What's the hurry, Bruno?' Huntley demanded. 'You could have hurt the lady.'

He cowed, ducking his head like a scolded child. 'I'm sorry,' he said again.

'All right,' Huntley's voice was softer at once. 'What did you come to tell me?'

'Nickel come by while I was eating. He was looking for the lady's guard, that Scotty feller.'

'Why did Nickel want to see him?'

'Them fellows he's been searching for are at the gate. Nickel said he was gonna help him arrest them.'

'The Polson brothers are here?' Amy was frantic. 'They're at the gate?'

'Along with a couple more guns. Gonna be five against Nickel and Scotty.'

'What?' Huntley and Amy both shouted the same word at the same time.

'I seen Cyrus following Nickel, so he is probably gonna help. If you want, I'll go help them too.'

'We have to stop this!' Amy cried. 'Three men against five cold-blooded murderers? Scotty will be killed!'

But gunfire erupted in the night. It was too late to stop the fight!

★   ★   ★

Whitney hadn't stopped to consider the rashness of his actions. He had been hurt and angry at seeing Amy come out of Huntley's bedroom looking as if she had . . . they had . . . He couldn't even think rationally about it.

When they approached the gate, five men were standing there. The guards had taken their horses to one side, but the men watching the gate were not regulators. They were told to detain the Polson brothers until Nickel arrived. Their job was done.

Nickel was in the center, with Whitney to the left and Cyrus to the right. They walked until they were less than thirty steps apart. 'Take the two on your side — I've got the pair in the middle,' Nickel spoke out of the corner of his mouth to Whitney. 'The end one on the right is your meat, Cyrus.'

'Leave me some scraps when you're done,' Cyrus replied. 'The first one is going down hard and fast.'

When Nickel stopped, so did Whitney and Cyrus. It was Whitney who addressed the group. 'You boys are under arrest for murder and horse-stealing.'

'What'n hell are you talking about?' one of the Polson boys yelped. 'This here's a safe haven! Ain't no law can touch us here.'

'You kilt my friend's brother and stole his herd,' Nickel piped up in reply. 'I'm hoping you don't opt to be arrested. Be less trouble to bury you than putting you in jail.'

'Who're you?' the man snarled back. 'And where is Milt Dewey?'

'Milt is rotting under six feet of dirt,' Whitney spoke up. 'You filthy scum aren't going to shoot and burn anyone else alive!'

There was no count, no one yelled *Draw!*, yet everything turned to chaos in an instant.

Each man was primed for a war — all eight grabbed for their guns at once — and the night was lit up by muzzle flashes and explosions. As guns blasted away, a dozen lead missiles sought their targets.

Whitney was handy with a gun, but slow compared to Nickel. He heard the man fire before he even cleared leather. His two opponents were both as quick as Whitney, but he was determined to make his shots count. A bullet whizzed past his ear and another kicked up dirt at his feet.

Whitney shut out the rest of the fight, making certain of his first shot. It knocked over one of the Polson brothers, hitting him squarely in the chest. He thumbed the hammer on his gun to get off another round, but something hit him high on the left side, nearly spinning him around. He maintained his focus and got off a second shot. The bullet was off line but hit the man in the thigh. It brought him down to his knees, but it failed to stop his return fire.

Bodies were spinning and falling; the gunfire was a roar like being caught inside a cloud during a thunder storm. Cyrus grunted and Nickel continued to fire guns with both hands. Cries split the night, yells of agony ripped from dying throats.

Whitney abruptly realized he was down on one knee. His gun was almost too heavy to lift. A sudden pain rocked his right side, but it wasn't enough to knock him over. He found his target, the second Polson brother, holding his free hand over his wounded leg and still trying to aim his smoking gun. His efforts ended with a pull of the trigger — not his, but Whitney's — and the shot was accurate. The bullet caused a tiny puff of fine powdery dust when it entered the man through his shirt pocket. The killer was knocked over on to his back . . . while Whitney fell forward on to his face.

The taste of dirt was in Whitney's mouth. There was a ringing in his ears, but the gunfire had ended. Even as a black pool beckoned him to dive in, he heard Nickel's voice.

'Damn, them boys came to the party prepared to dance.'

★ ★ ★

Whitney became aware of the light — it hurt his eyes. He was conscious of a sickeningly sweet smell, reminding him of a surgeon's work station. In his ears

was the sound of a woman's voice
. . . but it was not Amy.

'Well,' the feminine voice spoke,
sounding very close, 'are you going to
wake up, or do I throw your supper
away?'

It was a battle won, but the victory
caused a wave of nausea and a searing
fire to burn along his ribs and up
between his left shoulder and neck.
Whitney saw the owner of the voice. It
was Belva, the doctor's lady friend.

'Had us worried for a time there,
young man,' she said. 'If it hadn't been
for my Ralph, you would be singing
with the angels now.'

'Reckon they didn't let me in because
one of them had probably heard how I
can't carry a tune.'

She laughed, warm, rich and genuine. 'I knew I was going to like you.'

'How about the others?' he asked,
swallowing the momentary nausea.

'Buried six men this morning.'

'Six?'

'Mr Nickel didn't get so much as a

scratch, but Mr Cyrus was killed. I'm very sorry. He must have been a good friend to stand with you against such odds.'

'Where's — '

'Miss Cole?' she guessed. 'She stayed up all night and all day with you. I made her go get some sleep.'

He turned his head, able to see he was in a small room. 'Where am I?'

'Oh, Mr Huntley had them construct three rooms like this when the pharmacy was built. It serves as the only hospital within a hundred miles.'

Whitney was able to sit up with Belva's help. He could eat by himself that way. While consuming a few bites of tasty beef stew, he spied a notepad lying on the small table next to his bed.

'What's that?'

'I believe it is the next adventure of Tornado Tess,' Belva said. 'Amy was working on it while waiting for you to wake up. I can't imagine why she didn't take it with her.'

He gave a nod and finished his meal.

When he was done Belva said good-night and left the candle burning on the table by his bed. Whitney was not sleepy, having been unconscious for nearly twenty hours. He picked up the notepad and flipped it to the opening page.

'*Tornado Tess and the Mystery at Franklin's Fortress!*' he began.

★ ★ ★

Amy had breakfast with Huntley, the final meal she would be having with him. Once finished, she took his hand between her own and told him she appreciated what a great friend he'd been during her stay. He made it clear she was welcome to return at any time and they parted company.

It was with some trepidation she went to visit Whitney. She had left the book so he might understand the truth of the situation. She had always been better at writing than actually dealing with emotional issues. Taking a deep breath, she pushed open the door to Whitney's room. When he smiled at her, she knew he understood.

'Belva said you woke up last night,' she greeted him.

'Yeah, baby that I am, I let a couple little scratches knock my socks off.'

'Do you know about Cyrus?'

'Yes,' he answered, 'do *you* know about Cyrus?'

'Nickel gave me the telegram. I spoke to Jason but he didn't know anything about it.'

'Did you learn anything more?'

'Seems Cyrus Lowe's cousin is a policeman over in Colorado Springs. His cousin told Cyrus about the wife-abuser and how he wished there was something he could do.' She took a breath. 'You know it is almost impossible to get a divorce, and his cousin was worried the drunk might kill his wife while in one of his jealous rages.'

'So Cyrus shot the wife-abuser and framed the doctor, causing the doctor to flee here for Huntley. He was doing two favors at one time.'

'Mr Nickel said he was like that. He always wanted to do for his friends.'

Whitney bobbed his head. 'He joined us in the fight because Nickel was in it. He had no reason to risk his own life, but he stood by his friend.'

'The telegraph message was still something of a surprise.' She shrugged her shoulders. 'Kind of made a joke of all of my detective skills. All we needed to do was check to find out the charges had been dropped.'

'You solved the case,' Whitney said. 'Can't ask for a better result than that. Have you told Belva and Doc?'

'They were both relieved and amazed. If they had only stuck around for the hearing, the confession Cyrus left for the judge cleared Doctor Lyndell.'

'He had no reason to not tell the truth, other than that he could no longer go into Colorado without a warrant hanging over his head. No one was going to come to arrest him here.'

Amy moved over to stand at the

bedside. 'Did you read my story?'

'I skipped over some of it, other than when Tess and Flash McCord were together,' he said. 'I rather enjoyed those parts.'

'Then you believe me when I say nothing happened between Mr Huntley and me? I know how it must have looked, but — '

'Taking the belt to his pants might take some explaining, but I figure it was so you could outrun him. Man can't run very fast holding up his trousers.'

She laughed. 'The whole thing was much more innocent than it looked and sounded.'

'I believe you.'

Amy sighed her relief and he changed the subject.

'Truth is, I'm more concerned about how I missed out on the *second* time we kissed,' he declared, displaying a frown. 'It sounded like something a man wouldn't soon forget.'

'That was Tess and McCord,' she advised him, feeling her face go warm with embarrassment, 'not you and me.'

'My point exactly,' he said. 'When do I get that second kiss?'

'You read the ending,' she teased.

'About Tess actually marrying a man so they can work as partners?'

'Think it'll sell?' she wanted to know. 'It'll be a first for Tess.'

'Lean down here and I'll give you my unprofessional opinion.'

Amy stooped over the bed to kiss Whitney lightly, but he wrapped his good arm around her and she ended up lying almost on top of him.

'Careful!' she exclaimed. 'Your injuries!'

But he kissed her until she was out of breath, then smiled up at her. 'Damn, that hurts better than anything I ever felt before.'

'I'll expect a wedding as soon as you're up and around.'

'Nickel tells me there's a preacher in town, and he's agreed to be my best man.'

Amy laughed. 'Belva said the same

thing when I asked if she would stand up with me!'

They kissed once more and Amy wondered, *Now what kind of trouble can Tornado Tess get into with a husband . . . and possibly a child or two in tow?*

THE END

We do hope that you have enjoyed reading this large print book.

Did you know that all of our titles are available for purchase?

We publish a wide range of high quality large print books including:
Romances, Mysteries, Classics
General Fiction
Non Fiction and Westerns

Special interest titles available in large print are:
The Little Oxford Dictionary
Music Book, Song Book
Hymn Book, Service Book

Also available from us courtesy of Oxford University Press:
Young Readers' Dictionary
(large print edition)
Young Readers' Thesaurus
(large print edition)

For further information or a free brochure, please contact us at:
Ulverscroft Large Print Books Ltd.,
The Green, Bradgate Road, Anstey,
Leicester, LE7 7FU, England.
Tel: (00 44) 0116 236 4325
Fax: (00 44) 0116 234 0205

Other titles in the
Linford Western Library:

LANIGAN AND THE
SHE-WOLF

Ronald Martin Wade

Silas Cutler hires Shawnee Lanigan to track down the bank robbers who abducted his eighteen-year-old daughter, Sara Beth. The ruthless 'La Loba' leads the all female gang. When he tracks the outlaws down, he's staggered to discover the real reason for the kidnapping . . . Forced to report his failed rescue mission, he takes work supervising security for a mining operation. Lanigan unveils a plot and ultimately faces a vengeful mob — aware that they can't all make it out alive . . .